"I promise I'll go to a doctor."

"You had better or I'll see that you don't dance again." Anger distorted Casmir's features.

Marta stared at him, speechless with fury and fear, thinking of the eager ballerinas waiting to take her place. A wild thought whirled into her mind. "It's Cynthia, isn't it? You're going back to her."

"I do not see what difference it would make to you," he said flatly. "You and I are not lovers."

Marta had actually forgotten they were not the loving couple they pretended to be. They had grown so close....

"Or have you wanted me all along, Marta?"

She could feel her mouth trembling. "No," she whispered.

"I do not believe you." He wrapped his hand around the back of her neck and s

"I thir

dish

D1316011

Books by Claire Harrison

HARLEQUIN PRESENTS

These books may be available at your local bookseller.

Don't miss any of our special offers. Write to us at the following address for information on our newest releases.

Harlequin Reader Service
P.O. Box 52040, Phoenix, AZ 85072-2040
Canadian address: P.O. Box 2800, Postal Station A,
5170 Yonge St., Willowdale, Ont. M2N 6J3

CLAIRE HARRISON

one last dance

Harlequin Books

TORONTO • NEW YORK • LONDON
AMSTERDAM • PARIS • SYDNEY • HAMBURG
STOCKHOLM • ATHENS • TOKYO • MILAN

Light as a swallow in full flight she joined in the dance, and to the sound of cheers and shouting danced as she had never danced before. Her delicate feet seemed to be cut by sharp knives, but the anguish of her heart was so great that she did not feel the pain at all. She knew that this was the last evening she was to see the Prince....

The Little Mermaid by Hans Christian Andersen

———————◆———————

Harlequin Presents first edition March 1985
ISBN 0-373-10769-2

Original hardcover edition published in 1984
by Mills & Boon Limited

Copyright © 1984 by Claire Harrison. All rights reserved.
Philippine copyright 1984. Australian copyright 1984.
Except for use in any review, the reproduction or utilization of
this work in whole or in part in any form by any electronic,
mechanical or other means, now known or hereafter invented,
including xerography, photocopying and recording, or in any
information storage or retrieval system, is forbidden without
the permission of the publisher, Harlequin Enterprises Limited,
225 Duncan Mill Road, Don Mills, Ontario, Canada M3B 3K9.

All the characters in this book have no existence outside the
imagination of the author and have no relation whatsoever to
anyone bearing the same name or names. They are not even
distantly inspired by any individual known or unknown to the
author, and all the incidents are pure invention.

The Harlequin trademarks, consisting of the words
HARLEQUIN PRESENTS and the portrayal of a Harlequin,
are trademarks of Harlequin Enterprises Limited and are
registered in the Canada Trade Marks Office; the portrayal
of a Harlequin is registered in the United States Patent
and Trademark Office.

Printed in U.S.A.

CHAPTER ONE

MARTA COLE opened her eyes, turned over on to her back and stared up at a strange ceiling, one washed with early morning light and the occasional flicker of a shadow as the curtain at the window moved in the breeze. She looked up at it for a long time and then put her forearm across her eyes as if she could blot the sight from her eyes. She felt despair wash over her in great waves, and her insides felt as if their substance had been scooped out, leaving her empty, hollow, worthless. She had done what she had said she would never do, not even when she was at her loneliest and lowest point, not even when Blaine's death had seemed to be her own, not even when her room had felt like a jail cell, its four walls blank and looming, the silence louder than any voice could have been, the weight of it pressing against her ears.

The man next to her shifted slightly, the bed sheets rustling as he moved. She could only see a glimpse of his profile; an unshaven cheek, dark lashes against cheekbones, dark hair tousled on the pillow. He had been nice to her, sympathetic, understanding her pain as she had understood his. He was the victim of the present popularity of divorce, a man whose wife had left him, whose children barely knew him, whose unhappiness equalled hers in depth and breadth. They had comforted one another, she supposed. They had smiled at one another in the bar, had talked over drinks, had felt the intimate connection of sadness. And then she had gone with him to his apartment, not wanting to take him back to hers, knowing that what she sought in the bed and arms of a stranger was a burying of herself, complete oblivion.

It hadn't worked, of course. She hadn't been able to

7

forget who she was and that Blaine didn't exist anymore. She hadn't found anything more than a fleeting solace in another man's arms, and none of that had survived the night. She had used and been used, she had participated in a shallow encounter whose motions mimicked those of love, and what remained was the permanent ache lodged in her heart and a feeling of personal loathing. She had known that a one night stand wouldn't solve anything; she had known that seeking companionship in a bar was foolish and meaningless, but loneliness was a far more powerful enemy than she realised. It had made her leave the apartment, enter the darkened bar, drink more than she was accustomed to and laugh in the brittle fashion of a woman who is on the make. And the man on the bar stool next to her had recognised her precisely for what she was; a fellow sufferer, a kindred spirit in despair, another lost soul wandering through the dark maze of a personal hell.

Carefully, Marta slid out from under the sheets and dressed in the clothes that had fallen by the side of the bed; a grey skirt, sweater of soft rose wool and her beige raincoat. She put on her stockings but not her shoes so that she wouldn't make a sound as she left. She didn't want the man in the bed to wake; she didn't want to be forced into a conversation. She wanted to rush home, submerge herself in a hot bath and then go to the ballet studio where she could throw herself into the mindless and calming routine of barre exercises.

'You're leaving?'

Marta stood in the doorway to the bedroom and turned to face the bed. 'I have to go to work.'

He was leaning on his elbow. 'I come with breakfast,' he said. 'Bacon, eggs, cinnamon rolls, the works.' He gave a short, embarrassed laugh and Marta realised that he was no more accustomed to the polite exchange of a morning after than she was. She wondered if he was experiencing the same hollow feeling, the same sensation of self-hatred rising in him like bile.

She shook her head, her thick, black hair swaying against her shoulders. 'I have to rush. Really.'

His face was boyish and earnest. 'If you'd give me your phone number, then maybe we could. . . .'

'No, no. . . .' She took one more step out the door and then stood there hesitantly, her hands spread, palms up, in a helpless gesture. 'I'm sorry,' she began, knowing that she had nothing to give to him or to any other man while Blaine still lived inside her, the image of his face vivid in her mind and the memory of his lovemaking so strong that her body had failed her in a stranger's arms. 'So . . . sorry.' And with that, Marta fled from the apartment, her shoes in her hands, her stockinged feet making swift padding sounds as she ran down the corridors and stairs. She ran as if devils were after her, her legs shaking, her heart banging in her chest. When she was finally out of the building and standing on the pavement, she stopped to catch her breath, her chest heaving in fits and starts.

Passers-by looked at her with curiosity and she stepped back into the protecting niche of a doorway, the harsh feel of the pavement beneath her feet reminding her that she was not wearing shoes. She leaned against the doorway and, with fingers that quite literally shook like leaves, Marta put her shoes back on. Then she took a deep breath, stood up and clenched her hands at her sides to stop their quivering. No one was watching her now, and she slipped into the crowd of pedestrians; a tall, slender figure walking quickly, eyes blinking to keep back the tears, her long, dark hair rippling in the morning breeze.

The studio hummed with the sound of voices and the occasional trill of music as the pianist warmed up his fingers before company class began. It was a large room with walls lined with barres and mirrors and a smooth wooden floor. Dancers stood at the barres, bending and stretching, their choice of clothing as colourful as a rainbow and occasionally bizarre. Mismatched leg warmers, pinned-together leotards, tights with ladders, drooping sweatshirts and rolled-up exercise pants were generally the order of the day, although one or two dancers were pristine in new, black outfits.

Marta slipped quietly into the room and took her accustomed place at the barre, thankful for the noise and bustle, for the everyday quality of the studio that allowed her, for a short while, to be her normal self and to forget what she had done the night before. Like most of the others she wore several layers of disreputable clothing that she would strip off as class went on; a man's grey sweatshirt with cut-off sleeves, blue-and-white stiped leg warmers over black tights, a red leotard with a white scarf serving as a belt and a pair of scuffed pink point shoes with fraying ribbons. Her hair was pulled back into a bun and she wore a sweatband around her forehead.

She took hold of the barre and flexed her feet while next to her, Sandra, another member of the corps, made a deep plié and groaned.

'Can you hear my knees pop?' she asked. 'They're positively symphonic this morning.'

Marta looked at her and smiled. 'Can't hear a thing.' Sandra was one of the few members of the company that she had got to know. Because they were the same height, they tended to be put together. They stood next to one another in the long line of swans in *Swan Lake*; they were Spanish dancers in the *Nutcracker*; Wilis in *Giselle*.

Sandra leaned backwards, holding on to the bar with one hand while the other reached over her head in an arc. She was dark and, like Marta, almost too tall to be a ballet dancer. They had similar figures—slender and high-breasted with long, shapely legs. The resemblance between them, however, stopped at their faces. Marta's was oval, slightly pointed at the chin with small, even features and eyes the blue of the tropical sea, their length fringed with dark lashes. Sandra's face was rounder, her eyes were brown and her nose was prominent. But she had a wide smile that seemed to erase the plainness of her features and, when she danced, she was so lithe and weightless that Marta was sure that audiences never noticed her face.

'Have you heard the gossip?' Sandra asked in a low voice.

Marta shook her head as she put one foot up on the barre, pointed her foot and leaned her torso towards her knee, making all the muscles that ran up the back of her leg shriek in protest. 'Uh-uh,' she said.

'The grapevine says that Carrie Moore is pregnant.'

'Oh,' Marta said, straightening up slowly.

The implications of the prima ballerina of the Manhattan Ballet Company being pregnant were many and manifold. Carrie Moore danced every important role and was partner to Casmir Rudenko, the leading male dancer. They were one of the company's most important drawing cards, a couple who matched one another in an unlikely but dramatic and exciting way. Casmir was big, blond and exuberant with a dancing style that was muscular and theatrical. He was famous for the power of his leaps and jetés; his ability to mime; his seemingly effortless strength. Carrie, on the other hand, was delicate, petite and stunningly beautiful with long, honey-brown hair and slanted amber eyes. She had an ethereal quality to her, and critics swore that she seemed to float on the stage. Marta could remember watching them dance in *Romeo and Juliet* and thinking how their striking differences in style, physique and looks merely served to emphasise the uniqueness of each.

Carrie's pregnancy would leave Casmir without a partner and the company without its main female dancer. It would leave a space open at the top of the hierarchy and that meant that a shuffling of positions would occur. Every ballerina in the company would be praying that she would be the one to take Carrie's place. In the corps, hearts would beat hopeful. The very young dancers, the 'baby ballerinas', would dream of being recognised, of being snatched away from the anonymity of numbers to the spotlight of stardom. The older dancers, those who had been in the corps longer, would be warier, knowing that they had been passed over before and that their chances were not as great. Sandra was one of the latter, but Marta could see a wistfulness in her expression, a hoping that this time she would finally traverse that enormous gap between corps member and soloist.

Marta herself had no such illusions. Although she was new to the company, she was not a young dancer. She had spent several years in a regional ballet in upstate New York where she had danced all the choice parts and been celebrated, fêted and adored. She knew what it was like to be the doll in *Coppelia*, the young girl in *La Fille Mal Gardée*, Princess Aurora in *Sleeping Beauty*. Her dancing in the Rose Adagio had even garnered her praise in a national magazine, and although she had realised that she was a big fish in a small pond, it had seemed quite possible that New York or Paris or London would beckon and she would be welcomed, as a soloist, into one of the major dance companies.

The dream had, of course, been shattered by the accident; that dream as well as others, and Marta had spent the last two years putting her life back into some semblance of order, some type of routine where she could get up in the morning and manage all the small domestic details of existence. But the climb back to health had been a long one; her spirit had been as broken as her legs, and like them had never properly healed. Blaine was rarely out of her mind, and she often danced with sharp, shooting pains in her back and upper legs. Marta was sure that she had lost the lyricism of movement that had once been her hallmark, and she didn't think there was any chance that she would rise higher than the corps. She had, therefore, set her sights much lower than the other ballerinas. For Marta it was enough that she was dancing again and had the competence to perform with a professional company. For a while, it had looked as if she'd never dance again.

'I wonder who he'll choose,' Sandra added.

'Who?'

'Casmir. He'll have to pick another partner.'

'Céline?' Marta suggested, glancing at a young ballerina across the room who was reputed to be a favourite of Gregory Dunne, the ballet master.

Sandra gave a small snort. 'She wouldn't suit him at all. She's too athletic. No, my bet is on Cynthia.'

'She's too young.' Cynthia Donleavy had joined the ballet company only a few months before. She was a tiny dancer with long red hair and a pixiesh face; freckles played along her snub nose and she had wide, green eyes that looked perpetually astonished.

'Rumour also has it,' Sandra began, her voice lowering into a conspiratorial note, 'that ... oops, speak of the devil.'

Marta glanced at Sandra and then looked to the doorway where Casmir had appeared. He was a tall man, his head almost touching the top of the sill, his blond hair gleaming in the overhead light. His face was not handsome in a classical sense, but was a striking and masculine arrangement of planes and angles—a broad forehead, high slavic cheekbones, a wide mouth and strong, square jaw. He wore a dark blue leotard that left his shoulders and arms bare. Powerful muscles moved beneath his skin as his hands gestured; he was speaking to Gregory Dunne who ran the company as ballet master.

'You think I should go to the west coast?' he asked, his deep voice rolling with Russian inflections. 'It will take a month out of the Nutcracker rehearsals.'

Gregory nodded emphatically. He was small, rotund, bald as a billiard ball and a bundle of nervous energy. 'You've got the part down cold and, besides, the contract for the San Francisco company is a good one. You have nothing to lose.'

'I do not like dancing with strange companies.'

Gregory grabbed the ever-present cigar out of his mouth and waved his arms frantically in the air. 'Don't think like that. It's a great opportunity. They'll love you in San Francisco.'

Casmir seemed about to offer a rebuttal when Carrie walked up to the two men and began to speak to them in a low voice that didn't carry to Marta's side of the studio. She was slender and delicate-looking despite the fact that she was wearing a man's T-shirt and a pair of exercise pants that bagged at her hips.

'She doesn't look pregnant to me,' Marta said speculatively. 'Maybe your grapevine is going a bit wild.'

Sandra gave her a withering look. 'Is the moon not made of stone? Are point shoes not torture instruments? Come on, Marta. Has the grapevine ever been wrong?'

Marta pulled up a drooping leg warmer. 'I haven't been here long enough to know.'

'It's infallible,' Sandra insisted. 'The walls have ears, the doors leak and whispers sneak around the corridors. Believe me, if the grapevine says that she's pregnant, then it's true.'

Company class was always excruciating for Marta. Like all dancers, she stiffened overnight and had to stretch out again in the morning, but unlike the others, she never quite achieved a state of complete flexibility without pain. After the accident the doctors had told her that it would be a miracle if she ever danced again and, at first, she had concurred with their diagnosis, wondering despairingly, in the moments that she could rise above her memories and grief, what she would do with her life.

Finally, in desperation, she had turned her face from anything that reminded her of Blaine or ballet. Leaving the city where she had danced and been married, Marta moved into her mother's apartment in New York. She sold every bit of furniture that she and Blaine had owned and gave everything that belonged to him away. In the process of eliminating her old life, Marta had come adrift in her new one. She lost all sense of purpose or meaning; she slept for hours during the day and would read all night. In the rare times that she left the apartment she would go to the pictures where she sat numbly in the darkened cinema, almost oblivious to the passions enacted out before her on the screen.

Marta had not expected much help or comfort from her mother and Simone, as usual, had lived up to expectations. She was rarely home, flying frequently to Florida or California or Texas where she had friends. Simone had never been motherly. The Coles had always had enough money to enjoy the finer things in life and Simone had indulged in pleasure with great gusto and verve. Not even the death of Martin Cole had held her back for long. She liked to travel, to go to parties, to play golf, to visit health spas and resorts. Marta's place in her life had always been a small one, and even after the accident she had provided only the most minimal sympathy and pity, leaving for Palm Springs a month after Marta had moved in. Still, it was Simone that Marta could thank for her re-emergence as a dancer.

'Listen, doll,' she had said one afternoon as she breezed into Marta's room, tugging on a pair gloves. 'I'm off to Bendel's.'

'Have fun,' Marta had said, barely looking up from her book and taking another chocolate from the box that sat on her bedside table. When Simone was not travelling or visiting friends, she was shopping. She had accounts at every department store in New York.

'You know, Marta, you're getting fat. I'd get rid of the candy.'

This time Marta looked up. 'Fat?' she echoed.

'Positively corpulent,' Simone said with a delicate turning up of her nose. 'It doesn't become you.' She glanced at the mirror over Marta's dressing table and smoothed down the waves of her pale red hair. Simone prided herself on her looks and her figure. She was a well-preserved fifty, keeping herself youthful with exercise, diet and hundreds of small bottles of creams and cosmetics. 'Do you want anything while I'm gone?'

It was a rhetorical question and Marta knew better than to ask her mother for anything. 'No thanks, I'm fine.'

'I won't be home for dinner. I'm meeting the Graves at the club.'

'That's okay.'

'And don't wait up. I'll probably be late.'

'All right.'

After Simone left, Marta put down her book, got off the bed and went to stand in front of the mirror. She had not looked at herself in a long time, and she did not have any sense of who she was or how she was supposed to appear. What she saw in her reflection was a tired woman, looking older than her twenty-six years, whose hair hadn't been washed often enough and whose face had taken on an extra chin and a fleshy look around the mouth and nose. She did not resemble the smiling and pretty woman that Blaine had married or the dancer whose slender face and body had adorned posters for the Syracuse Dance Company. She looked like no one Marta had ever seen before, and she suddenly felt disgust at the heaviness of her body and her own dull lethargy.

With a sense of determination that she had not had in months, Marta walked over to the bed, picked up the half-empty box of chocolates and dumped it into the waste paper basket. She made the bed, pulled open the drawer of her chest of drawers where she kept her dance clothes and dug her point shoes out of the bottom of her wardrobe. She did not know if it was possible for the old Marta to be resurrected, and she had no idea if she would be able to dance again, but she had to try. Gritting her teeth, she put tights over legs that had suddenly gone wobbly and pulled ballet shoes over feet that protested with pain. The doctors had said that she would never dance again, but maybe they were wrong. Maybe if she worked hard enough, it would all come back to her like a dream she had once dreamt where she danced across the stage, a bird in flight, swooping, turning, soaring, every motion effortless and smooth and beautiful.

And she had done it, Marta thought, catching a glimpse of herself in the mirror at the other side of the studio as company class began. She had lost the weight, strengthened her legs and feet and become a dancer once again. The struggle had been an uphill one of strenuous dieting and exercising until she dropped from exhaustion, her legs shaking with effort, her teeth aching from the way she would clench them. The doctors had been right in a way; she would never be the dancer she had once been, but she was willing to sacrifice a great deal in order to be back in a world that she knew and loved. Since she had been five years old Marta had wanted to be a ballerina; nothing else had mattered to her as much as dancing. Not even Blaine, although she had loved him she had thought as much as a woman could love a man.

As she looked into the mirror a pair of blue eyes caught hers and, startled by the sudden intrusion into her thoughts, Marta quickly looked away, concentrating on the music and ballet master's commands. 'And tendu, tendu, plié, plié. Up, stretch, down and bend. Tendu, glissé. . . .' When she finally got the nerve to glance at the mirror again he was no longer looking at her but seemed also to be concentrating on his feet, his broad chest beginning to gleam with sweat, its gold hairs turning dark.

She wondered why Casmir had been watching her; he had never bothered to notice her before, and she had always thought she was far too insignificant to capture the attention of one of the company's most important dancers. He didn't seem very interested in women actually; she never saw him with any other dancer than Carrie who was, if the grapevine was correct, a very happily married woman and mother. Marta had heard that Casmir was a widower, married for only a brief time to a woman who had been killed during a mugging near Central Park. It was a tragic story, but she could only speculate if Casmir had grieved as she did; if he felt as lost without his wife as she felt without Blaine.

The occasional gossip that she was privy to stated that, before his marriage, Casmir had slept with most of the corps de ballet, displaying a gusto and appetite that had defied the imagination. He would no sooner be intimate with one dancer than he was already flirting with the next, his Russian charm bowling them over like so many ten pins. Marta could understand the attraction he had for women. He was good looking, utterly masculine and very, very successful. His woman of the moment would have basked in the reflection of his limelight, his glory extending to her like a golden mantle.

'Turn,' Sandra hissed.

'Sorry,' Marta whispered contritely, realising that she had been day-dreaming. She turned around so that she was facing away from the mirror and now could see the muscular play along Casmir's back and shoulders. But she resolutely looked away, determined to concentrate on her exercises. Casmir meant nothing to her, and she did not see their paths crossing in the future. He was a star, she was very low on the totem pole and there was no reason why that state of affairs would ever change.

In the dressing room late that afternoon the air hummed with tension and excited conversation. Gregory had let it be known that new assignments would be posted before the end of the day, and the grapevine had buzzed all afternoon with hints, rumours and speculation. Carrie, it was said, was two months pregnant and had decided to rest out this pregnancy the way she had the last one when she'd had the twins. No one knew precisely why she had decided to give up dancing so early but, according to one avid gossip, she had had a miscarriage before her wedding to Alex Taylor and was afraid of having another one. That bit of news was greeted with much shaking of heads and raised eyebrows. It was the company's general consensus that Carrie had never played fast and loose with anyone and had always avoided romantic entanglements. One doubter pointed out that rumours had flown about Carrie and Casmir at one time, but another scoffed at that angle, insisting that only friendship had existed between the two dancers and that, besides, Casmir had got married to someone else.

One ballerina suggested that he had married on the rebound, but another who had been with the company for a long time insisted that he had married for love. It had been a true romance, she said, recalling how Casmir had pursued Bonnie Hughes, the company's publicity director. They had argued, fought and spit at one another like angry cats and, then, when Bonnie had finally succumbed to Casmir's exuberant charm . . . well . . . and the ballerina sighed with nostalgia, thereby letting the rest of them know that she had once been Casmir's lover and that the rumours of his past prowess had not been exaggerated.

'How did it feel to be in a cast of thousands?' someone asked a bit slyly, but the older ballerina was not to be baited. 'We considered it an exclusive club,' she said and they all laughed.

'Maybe he's got a girlfriend on the outside,' someone else said. 'He's lost interest in ballerinas.'

Several voices then chimed in with rebuttals and suggestions, theorising on the reasons behind the change in Casmir's personality.

'He isn't as happy as he used to be.'

'I heard he went a little berserk after his wife died.'

'He took up drinking.'

'Gregory had to cut off his voka supply so he'd come to class.'

'Actually,' someone near Marta said in sotto voce to her neighbour as the group broke up and dancers began to leave the dressing room, 'a little bird told me that our most eminent male dancer has taken up with a certain Donleavy.

'No kidding!'

'They went to the movies one night and out to dinner

the next. I hear she has stars in her eyes and dreams of stardom in her head.'

'You mean they're——?'

The first ballerina shrugged. 'Who knows? But I don't think we've got a chance if she's in the running.'

'She's good, you know.'

'Not that good and not that experienced.'

'Casmir will teach her.'

They were both silent for a moment and the first one said, 'I'd give my eyeteeth to be in her shoes.'

'Me too,' the second said. 'I'd kill for the chance.'

Marta tuned out the voices as she peeled off her tights and put them in her bag. She did not really want to discuss Casmir's sex life or hear the gossip. She kept her own life very private, not wanting her own tragedy to become part of the company's stories and speculation. Almost everyone knew about the accident and Blaine's death; they were events that were impossible to hide because dance magazines and newsletters had carried the story when it occurred. There had been a rush of interest in her when she had first joined the company, but her aloofness had cooled the most curious and others had learned, to their discomfort, that she was not to be drawn out. Sandra was the closest that Marta had to a friend in the company, but even that was a misnomer. They were merely acquaintances; their conversation never went beyond the trivial.

Her coolness had not been deliberate; it was compounded of shyness, unhappiness and reticence. The contentment of others made her feel like an outsider, and Marta found it difficult to be warm and friendly. Loneliness had settled in like a permanent guest; a damaging, piercing loneliness. She had never known that it was possible to feel so alone. She was a solitary island in crowds; a nonentity in her mother's life. All the joy that Marta had once felt, the light-hearted spirits that had once made her well-liked and sought after seemed to have evaporated into the air like thin whiffs of smoke. She could recall how Blaine had loved her laughter, her playfulness, her lack of seriousness, and she winced inwardly at the memory. *That* Marta no longer existed; *she* came from another time when life stretched ahead like a gleaming filament, when every promise that life could offer seemed to be fulfilled, and love had tangled her in its soft and velvet bonds.

The hallway outside the dressing room was crowded with dancers dressed in street clothes and carrying duffel bags. There was whispering and bursts of nervous laughter as they waited for the notice of assignments to be posted. Marta, seeing that she had no reason to stick around, tried to make her way down the hall to the front door, but her passage was blocked by a sudden grouping of people as the door to the director's office was flung open, and Gregory emerged, brandishing a smoking cigar and several long sheets of paper.

'Okay, folks,' he said. 'Give me a little space.'

Marta was pressed against the wall as the crowd surged back, giving Gregory room to make it to the bulletin board. He put up the papers with great fanfare, hitting the thumbtacks with a small hammer and complaining whenever someone got too close. When he was finally finished, he turned and faced them, blocking everyone's view of the lists.

'These are the assignments for our fall tour,' he said. 'We've had to do a bit of juggling and pasting to put them together. Now, the reason for this is that Carrie Moore has gone and got herself in trouble again.' He waited until the laughter had died down. 'The kid will be due around Christmas and we're expecting her back for the spring season so normal casting will resume after the *Nutcracker*. In the meantime, some of you will get a chance to show off your stuff to the folks out there in the boondocks. We'll be hitting the northeast this year; Hartford, Boston, Syracuse, Providence and an assortment of other places you'll wish you'd never heard of.'

There were the usual groans. The company tour was always as tiring as it was exhilarating. The small town audiences were thrilled when the company came, applauded enthusiastically and gave the dancers front-page coverage in papers whose titles included the word *Gazette* or *Leader* or *Dealer*. On the other hand, the small towns had old hotels with antiquated plumbing or motels with ticky-tacky decor and restaurants with indifferent service and menus that were restricted to fried and fattening food. But touring was necessary; it introduced culture to backwater towns, inspired interest in ballet and brought prestige to the company. Marta looked forward to leaving Manhattan for a while; she needed a change of scenery, she needed to get away from the apartment and, above all, she needed to be so busily involved in her professional life that the loneliness in her private one wouldn't drive her to. . . .

'Now, don't trample me,' Gregory said, waving his cigar in a half-circle and forcing the closest rank of dancers back a step. 'And if you have any complaints, the suggestion box will be posted by the doorway.'

That brought a few laughs because there was no such thing as a suggestion box, and everyone knew that, once the assignments were posted, there wasn't a chance that the company management would make a change. Dancers for solo roles were picked by the ballet master and the director, and they would not brook any interference. A dancer who thought she deserved to be cast in a role but had not been had no choice but to quit or shut up. There was nothing in the least bit democratic about a ballet company.

As the crowd surged forward, Marta once again began working her way down the hallway. She had almost made it to the turn down another corridor when she heard her name called out in exclamation and then a buzz of excited, questioning voices.

'I don't believe it!'

'Wasn't she the one who . . .?'

'I never would have thought. . . .'

Marta stood stock-still, her body half-turned as if to leave, a sudden disbelief making her frown, the dark wings of her eyebrows pulling together. A figure came rushing out of the crowd—Sandra, looking incredulous and stunned. 'Well, congratulations,' she said. There was a twisted look to her mouth that Marta suddenly perceived as jealousy.

'Congratulations? For what?'

'You didn't guess? I wondered if you were playing dumb.'

'Guess what?'

'Come with me.'

Sandra took Marta's arm and dragged her back down the hallway and through the group of dancers who parted before them like the Red Sea. Marta caught a glimpse of faces that held a mixture of expressions— astonishment, envy, outright dislike. There was one face that caught her attention as she passed by; a mouth clenched tightly together, a freckled nose, green eyes that were swimming with tears. It was Cynthia Donleavy, Marta saw, whose hopes had been shattered, and she remembered the gossip in the dressing room— Cynthia's dates with Casmir, the speculation that they were sleeping together, the assumption that she would be his partner. Cynthia had obviously believed it herself, and Marta had a quick flash of pity for her. She too had been young once and very hopeful.

'There,' Sandra said, planting Marta right in front of the lists. 'Take a look at that.'

It was a few seconds before the letters unblurred and Marta could see the sheets clearly. Each one was titled with the name of a ballet, the soloists listed below. The company, she saw, was planning a number of ambitious programmes for the tour. The Nijinsky ballet, *Le Spectre de la Rose*, was one; there was *Sleeping Beauty*, a mammoth production that particularly appealed to audiences in small towns; and finally the pas de deux from *Le Corsaire*, an exotic dance between a pirate and a beautiful young girl. Marta's eyes moved from the titles to the names, and she blinked once before making the final connection. For each ballet, her name was paired with Casmir. She had been plucked from the corps and dropped, with no advance warning, into starring roles. And her understudy? Cynthia Donleavy.

CHAPTER TWO

MARTA was, of course, thrown into a whirlwind of activity following the announcement of ballets and roles. In addition to her regular class there were fittings, publicity events, rehearsals, rehearsals and more rehearsals; alone, with Casmir, under Carrie's instruction or Gregory's stern eye. Certain parts of *Sleeping Beauty* were familiar to Marta as her former dance company had performed them for its local audiences, but she had never learned the ballet in its entirety, and the two other ballets were unknown to her. And training for a starring role was different than rehearsing for the corps where a dancer could blend in with the others, her flaws not always discernible to the audience. Soloists danced in the spotlight, every misstep or mistake glaringly apparent.

Casmir came, however, to be a rock of strength and confidence. During their first rehearsal of the final pas de deux in the *Sleeping Beauty* they worked together in the studio, a record supplying them with the music. Casmir led Marta through the steps of the dance slowly until he was sure that she knew them and, when he lifted or moved her, she could sense his careful adjustment to her weight, her balance and her equilibrium. But his competence did not stop her from shying away from a leap and then, realising what she had done, leap too late. He caught her without a second to spare, saving her from an embarrassing and potentially painful fall, his hands strong and sure on her waist.

'I'm sorry,' she said, breathing hard as he turned her upright and lowered her to the floor. 'I'm a little nervous, I guess.' They were both sweating slightly, and Marta felt her torso sliding against the hard wall of

25

Casmir's chest. He wore only black tights and soft black shoes; the rest of him was bare, bronzed and glistening.

'You have partners who drop you?' Casmir asked. His hand lingered at the curve of her hip, his deep blue eyes scrutinised her face.

'Not actually dropped,' she said, 'but not quite held either.' Her partner at the Syracuse Dance Company had been talented but a weak performer. It had not stopped him from climbing to a starring role because good male dancers were hard to find, but he lacked the strength, the sophistication and the dedication that Casmir brought to partnering.

'Don't worry, I do not hurt you.'

Marta looked up into his eyes and then back away from him so that the hand that he held at her waist dropped to his side. She could see why so many women were fascinated by him, he had eyes that caressed and a voice that enfolded her in its warmth. 'I won't do it again,' she promised, and then aimed for a light tone, 'No more chickening out.'

He did not make an attempt to console her or touch her again, he merely gave her a casual, friendly shrug. 'Everyone makes mistakes, *lapushka*. Is par for the tab.'

Marta blinked. 'Don't you mean for the course?' she asked in bewilderment.

His grin was ingenuous. 'I am dancer,' he said, 'not linguist.'

She learned to trust him implicitly, to throw herself in the air, knowing with utter confidence that his hands, his arms, his body would be there to support her as she came down. And he never manhandled her. Marta had had plenty of experience with partners whose fingers convulsively gripped her waist, leaving large black-and-blue marks, or whose hands almost pulled her arms out of their sockets. It was joy to dance with Casmir and, the more she relaxed when they moved together, the more she felt her own dancing improve. She felt some of the old lyrical grace that had earned her such praise.

And Casmir was only modestly temperamental. He had strong feelings about some of Gregory's interpretations, and he didn't hesitate to state opposing opinions. Marta had watched, with an astonished expression, while he and Gregory stormed at one another for fifteen minutes; Casmir throwing his hands up to the ceiling in disgust, his already less-than-idiomatic English coming apart at the seams. Russian, French and English words were mixed together helter-skelter while Gregory stamped, and puffed at his cigar. As soon as the battle was over, Casmir winning, Gregory compromising, Casmir threw his arms around the diminutive ballet master, twirled him in the air and kissed him on both cheeks. It was impossible, Marta saw, to be angry with Casmir for long.

It was hard not to like him, but Marta was wary. Company gossip, which had linked him strongly to Cynthia, now wavered on the indecisive. There was rumour of a jealous argument, of snide comments, of a tearful phone call. Marta tried to stay clear of the grapevine, but other dancers would not let her. Sandra had taken to dropping into her dressing-room (now that Marta had achieved a star rating, she no longer had to dress with the multitudes), curling up on the couch provided in one corner and chatting. Her initial jealousy of Marta had calmed to resignation, and her high spirits prevailed. During the weeks of rehearsals when Marta was feeling pre-performance jitters and terrified that her legs would act up, she discovered that Sandra's company was both enjoyable and relaxing. The other dancer was amusing, self-deprecating and knowledgeable. She made Marta laugh, and that was something Marta had not been able to do in a long, long time.

'This is a true story,' she said one afternoon as Marta carefully applied tincture of Merthiolate to her toes to toughen them. There were all sorts of remedies that dancers used to protect their feet from point shoes, but despite the careful care that Marta took of her points, she still got the occasional blister and sore.

'What is?' she asked idly.

'Well,' Sandra said, tucking her legs underneath her, 'one of the New York companies was travelling in the south, and the town they were visiting had really done a bang-up reception job.'

'What did they do?'

'Polished the stage floor.'

'Ouch,' Marta said with a dramatic wince. Polished floors made dancers slip and slide; most companies carried their own floor covering on tour as protection.

'In desperation, they sprinkled cleanser on the floor.' Cleanser!'

'It was great for the dancers, but the stuff got everywhere—in the orchestra, into the lighting, between the teeth of the conductor. . . .'

Marta laughed, 'Really,' she said.

'No joke.'

'Sometimes, I think you make these things up.'

Sandra raised a hand in protest. 'I am the soul of honesty and discretion.'

'Since when?'

'Since lunch—I mixed honesty and discretion into the tuna fish.'

Marta shook her head in mock-despair and bent over her toes again.

'I hear rehearsals for *Spectre de la Rose* are coming along well,' Sandra said.

'Casmir's amazing. Despite all those muscles, he can somehow give a feeling of . . . well, being the essence of a rose.' It was a ballet that had been choreographed as a showcase for a male dancer of extraordinary versatility. In it, a young girl falls asleep while holding a rose and, while she is dreaming, the spirit of the rose comes alive and dances with her. It was a romantic and sensual ballet, choreographed by Fokine for the famous dancer Nijinsky, and based on a French poem beginning, *'Je suis le spectre d'une rose, Que tu portais hier au bal. . . .'*

'I hear he's dropped Cynthia.'

'Let's not talk. . . .'

'You may be next.'

'Next what?'

'The next Casmir conquest.'

Marta shook her head firmly. 'I'm not inclined and neither is he. We're strictly working partners, that's all.'

Sandra looked disbelieving, 'Famous last words. I can't see you turning Casmir down. Have you noticed what that man looks like in a leotard?'

'Frequently and without interest.'

'You must be abnormal, Marta. I could fall for him in a second.'

'Not me,' Marta said. 'I'm afraid I'm impervious.'

Of course, it wasn't true at all, she thought after Sandra had left. Marta could not only see what Casmir looked like, she could feel him against her in positions only somewhat less intimate than that of a lover. His body was hard, every muscle defined beneath the fabric of his leotard, the depth of his chest accentuated by the leanness of hips and long legs. When she placed her hands on his shoulders, and she was up on point, their mouths were almost level, and Marta had found herself, much to her amazement, wondering what that mouth would feel like and dreaming about leaning just that slightest inch forward and placing her lips against his. She'd had to shake herself once or twice during rehearsal and concentrate on what Gregory was telling her. She had to remember that Casmir was, in actual fact, no more than a means to an end, the muscle that provided her with the ability to soar in the air, to stretch in long graceful lines. When he danced alone, he was magnificent, but when they danced together, he provided the showcase for her skill.

He was, however, a superb male specimen, and Marta could not seem to stop her body from reacting in ways that had not occurred to her with any other partners during her years in ballet. Perhaps Blaine's presence in her life had stopped her from amorous entanglements with other dancers; certainly, it was not uncommon for ballerinas to fall in love with their partners, but Marta had known Blaine since childhood, had dated him in high school and, between professional seasons with the Syracuse Dance Company, had married him. There had never been another man in her life, and she suspected, looking back, that she simply hadn't had time for romance. Her days had been filled with classes and rehearsals. If Blaine hadn't existed, she wasn't even sure she would have got serious about any man, particularly one outside the ballet world. She had been far too wrapped up in dancing to concentrate on anything as distracting as love.

But Blaine had somehow fitted smoothly into her schedule. While she was in training he finished his college degree and took a job as assistant manager at a local bank. He had accepted the premise of her life, that ballet was of prime importance, and filled in around the edges. Marta could remember the nights she'd come home from a rehearsal and found the shopping done, the washing done and dinner made and waiting, Blaine wrapped in an apron, his light-brown hair damp and curling on his forehead. How she had loved him! She'd rush through the door, throw her arms around his neck and praise him extravagantly. Hyperbole had been part of her life then; she saw everything in glamorous, exciting and larger-than-life terms. He was the best husband; she was going to be the best dancer; the Syracuse Dance Company was going to dazzle the world with its professionalism, its enthusiasm, its costumes, its dancers, its techniques, its. . . .

God, but she'd been young then. Young and innocent and naïve. She'd never known defeat or failure or a sexual caress that wasn't bestowed with love. She might not deny the physical attraction that Casmir held for her, but cynicism had grown along with experience. Marta deeply regretted the night she had spent with a stranger, but she had learned something important about herself as a result. She had learned that she was not a casual person that could take sex lightly, and had discovered that a loveless intimacy was shallow, unrewarding and incapable of filling the emptiness within her.

Neither she nor Blaine had had much sexual experience, but what they shared had been comforting and satisfying. Looking back, Marta had come to understand that she had taken his presence for granted when he was alive, never realising how much he had meant to her. She prayed that Blaine had guessed how she felt about him; she hoped that he had, in his quiet way, understood what lay beneath the surface of her smiles and impulsive hugs and breathless confidences. But she would, of course, never know if he had. Although the sharp edge of her grief had dissipated, Blaine's death had left her with this legacy of guilt. If only she hadn't been so busy rushing to and from the ballet studio, obsessed with her own life, if only she had taken a moment to analyse her own feelings, if only she had spoken—a thousand and one *if onlys* that no longer could be resolved. *That*, she had learned, was the most devastating fact about death; it was irrevocable and there was no turning back, no altering, no earning second chances to correct mistakes, to tell someone that you loved him . . . to make him happy.

Marta blinked, noticed that a ray of sunlight was cutting a deep angle across the top of her dressing table and realised how much time she had lost, thinking about the past. It was ground she had covered so many times before: unanswered prayers and futile wishes, a territory that had already dragged her down once into a bleak depression. She had to think about the future; calmly, coldly and with calculation. Casmir had made her his partner and given her a chance to show the world that she could be the dancer she had once hoped to be. Getting involved with him in a casual sexual way was strictly out of the question. His Russian exhuberance was appealing, his physical attractions strong, but Marta was wary and very careful. She knew just how vulnerable her heart was: it was far too fragile to be plucked and discarded in whim or caprice or carelessness.

Carrie Moore spent three afternoons a week with Marta running her through the steps to the *Le Corsaire* pas de deux and the opening scenes of *Sleeping Beauty*. She knew the music by heart and would hum as she showed Marta the movements. And, while she was kind and generous to a fault, she was also absolutely painstaking. They never went from one movement to the next until Marta had got the first one absolutely straight. They worked by themselves in one of the smaller studios and, on one particular afternoon, when the heat seemed to sizzle against the windows, Marta finally threw her hands up in disgust and slumped down a wall to a sitting position on the floor. Despite the brevity of her leotard, she was hot and sweating.

'What happened to the air conditioning?' she asked, lifting damp tendrils of black hair from her neck in a vain effort to get cool.

'They're working on it,' Carrie said, sitting down in a nearby chair. She didn't look hot at all. In fact, she looked quite composed in a T-shirt and shorts, her long swathe of honey-brown hair pulled into a tight bun. She glanced down at her waistline where her pregnancy had started to show and made a small grimace. 'You know, this is beginning to look like another set of twins.'

Marta gave her a weary grin. 'You don't believe in half-measures, do you?'

'Oh, I blame it on Alex,' she said lightly. 'Having more kids was his idea.'

'I wonder how you do it.'

'Do what? Oh, stay married, have babies and dance?' Marta nodded. 'It's a compromise really. I wasn't happy not having a family, and I wouldn't be happy just staying at home and taking care of children either. Alex is very supportive, I have a live-in housekeeper, and I've learned to slow down at times. I'll probably spend some of my pregnancy working on choreography. I love doing that.'

'How did you meet your husband?'

Carrie gave a little laugh and then blushed like a schoolgirl. 'In Florida, at a resort. It was . . . love at first sight, ridiculous as that may sound.'

'I don't know if it's ridiculous or not,' Marta said slowly. 'It's never happened to me.'

Carrie gave her an appraising look. 'You were married, weren't you?'

Marta leaned forward to tie up a loose ribbon on her point shoes. 'We were childhood sweethearts. Our families lived next door to one another.'

'I heard about the accident. I'm sorry; it must have been awful.'

Marta straightened up, flexed her shoulders and gave Carrie a small smile. 'I'm trying to put the past behind me.'

'Sometimes, that's best,' Carrie said softly, 'I can understand that.'

There was something about Carrie that inspired trust; she was open, gentle and sympathetic, and Marta suspected that she was reticent as well. Sandra would be the type to gossip to everyone in the company, but Carrie was above the ballet grapevine. Whatever was said in this room, would go no further.

'Why did Casmir choose me as his partner?' she asked.

Carrie threw her a surprised look. 'You don't know?'

'No. I'm not good enough, really.'

'You were a unanimous choice. We all thought you'd be suitable; myself, Gregory, and Casmir was particularly enthusiastic.'

It was Marta's turn to look astonished. 'I find that hard to believe.'

'But you have a lovely line,' Carrie said, 'and a great deal of grace.'

'But I'm not like you at all and. . . .'

'Casmir wasn't looking for someone like me,' Carrie said firmly. 'He needs a partner who will complement him in other ways, and the fact that we're so different will keep the critics from making comparisons. You and Casmir will look great together; you're dark and he's blond, you're both tall people—I bet you're almost six foot on point.'

'But ever since the accident. . . .'

'We've all noticed a tremendous improvement, Marta. Don't underestimate yourself; you deserve what you've been given.'

The compliments had the effect of making Marta tongue-tied. 'I'm . . . well, I can't help worrying about . . . I guess it's stage fright.'

Carrie leaned over and placed a gentle hand on her shoulder. 'Take it from me, Marta. You're going to do just fine. Really, I have great hopes for you; you may dance me right out of a job.'

Marta was horrified. 'No! I wouldn't think of that; I have no intentions of. . . .'

Carrie laughed. 'I'm not worried,' she said. 'Now, come to dinner at my place tonight. Alex is out of town, and I've invited Casmir as well. The dress is casual and we can talk shop for hours without boring a soul.'

'Well, I. . . .'

'I'll be disappointed if you don't come,' Carrie said warningly. 'I'll flunk you on your next arabesque.'

Marta smiled up at her. 'All right,' she said, 'I'll be there.'

Carrie's apartment was magnificently situated in a luxurious high-rise block overlooking Central Park, was beautifully decorated with contemporary furniture that featured grey leather, glass and bronze and was scattered with toys from one corner to the other. There were coloured plastic rings and building blocks on the dark grey living-room carpet, a wooden climbing gym with a small slide in the dining room and various trucks and cars dotting the hallway. Mark and Matthew were two-and-one-half years old, quick on their feet, curious, noisy, busy and adorable in the extreme. Both Carrie and her housekeeper were busy trying to round up both children for their baths when Marta arrived. Carrie, with a distracted air, welcomed Marta and suggested apologetically that she hide in the kitchen.

'The evening battle seems to be prolonged. I swear that the twins go haywire when Alex is gone.' Mark or Matthew, who was tucked under Carrie's arm, gave Marta an engaging, devilish grin, while he untied the bow that held his mother's apron strings together. Carrie swung him around so that they were nose to nose. 'Listen, buster, this is your last chance to remain in this family. Cuteness will only get you so far and, besides, you're about to be usurped by a baby sister, I hope.'

Mark or Matthew thought this was hilarious and, laughing with gusto, threw back his head with its cap of black curly hair.

Carrie gave Marta a helpless look. 'My advice? Make sure your children are beyond age three when they're born; that's the only answer.'

Marta found Casmir in the kitchen. He was cutting up celery into a large wooden salad bowl. He looked comfortable in Carrie's kitchen, sitting on a stool with one booted foot in a rung, dressed in a dark blue velour top and a pair of jeans. 'Radishes or green peppers?' he asked, glancing up at Marta.

'Green peppers.'

She was provided with a knife, a cutting board and a vegetable. 'An apron?' Casmir asked.

Marta glanced down at her white slacks and pale mauve blouse. 'I guess I'd better,' she said, accepting one from his outstretched hand.

Casmir twirled a knife in the air with a dramatic flourish, 'In my next life, I become a chef.'

'Do you believe in reincarnation?' she asked, tying the apron around her waist.

'Certainly. I was serf in Russia in my last life.'

'A peasant?' she asked disbelievingly as she began to slice the peppers.

'It was not for Casmir to work the soil. No, I was serf to the Tsar and Tsarina.'

'I see. You were important.'

'Of course. You think Casmir would not be important even in a previous life?' He took on a look of aggrieved insult.

'I thought the Hindus believed that you could even be an animal in a previous lifetime—maybe even a bug.'

'Marta, *milaya*, you may have been centipede in your former life, but do not suppose that fate intended me to crawl on six legs.'

'You danced for the Tsar.'

'Certainly not.' Casmir put down his knife and gave Marta an intense look from his slanted blue eyes. They were the colour of innocence, almost turquoise and fringed with golden lashes. 'I was lover to the Tsarina,' he added dramatically.

Marta hid a smile. 'Like that mystic? What was his name—Rasputin?'

'My ignorant *lapushka*,' Casmir said condescendingly, 'you make an insult. Rasputin was dirty slob; I was glorious lover. You must learn to make the difference.'

'Distinction,' she said. 'In English, we make distinctions.'

Casmir shrugged, picking up his knife and applying it to the celery again. 'I was the toast of all Russia.'

Marta willingly spun out the fantasy. 'Wasn't the Tsar jealous? It was his wife, after all.'

'It was a marriage of convenience not of love. They only sleep together for the children. That is the way of royalty.'

'I'm afraid I wouldn't know anything about that. I'm middle class through and through.'

'Bourgeois,' Casmir agreed as he dumped a handful of celery into the bowl. 'So—in my next life I have decided to become a great chef. After the love, what is there but food? I will wear a white apron and one of those magnifique hats. I preside over great Russian establishment; women will swoon over my sauces. . . .'

He was interrupted by Carrie, who entered the kitchen looking harassed but relieved. 'I think the troops are under control,' she said and then, glancing at the wooden bowl in front of Casmir, gave a slight frown. 'Are we only having a salad of celery and peppers?'

Casmir bowed with a flourish. 'We got carried away,' he said. 'The conversation was ... how do you say?— titillating.'

Marta and Carrie both looked bewildered and then gave one another amused looks. 'I think he means scintillating,' Marta said with a smile.

Carrie wrapped her arms around Casmir, who was looking hurt, and gave him a bear hug. 'Don't ever have those English lessons you keep threatening to take,' she said. 'You're fun just the way you are.'

The conversation during dinner was light-hearted and amusing. They talked about the company and gossiped about personalities. Carrie and Casmir relived some memorable ballets for Marta, recalling humorous mistakes and almost fatal misses. There was the time Carrie's skirt unravelled, its threads winding their way around Casmir's legs. There was the leap on a sloped stage in Atlanta that turned into a pratfall, and there was the miscue that brought Carrie out on stage prepared to leap into Casmir's arms only to find that, not only was he not there with her, he was not even in the wings.

'What did you do?' Marta asked.

'Made it up as I went,' Carrie said. 'It's a new art form—instant choreography.'

What they didn't talk about was anything serious or personal. Neither Casmir nor Carrie asked Marta anything more significant than her opinions on diets (the obsession of dancers), point shoes (what did she wear and how did they fit) and the New York dance scene (who was dancing with which company, what dancer was unhappy and ready to move, which company had a coveted engagement...). It was absorbing, fascinating and fun, and when Marta was ready to leave, she told Carrie how glad she was that she had come.

'Good,' Carrie said. 'It seems to me that you'd been in hiding and it was time to come out. Don't you think so, Casmir?'

'Marta is very mysterious,' he said, rolling his r's. 'I find out more about her on the way home.'

Marta gave him a surprised look. 'You don't need to walk me home. I live close by.'

Casmir shook his head. 'New York is too dangerous.'

'No, there's really no need,' Marta said, putting on a sweater and lifting her dark swathe of hair out of its neckline so that its wavy length hung on her shoulders. 'I'm used to being on my own.'

'I walk you,' Casmir said, and there was an unexpectedly grim look around his mouth that made Marta recall that his wife had been killed during a mugging. Most New Yorkers adjusted to the more dangerous aspects of the city with a nonchalant, fatalistic attitude, but she saw that Casmir did not and knew that, no matter how much she protested, he was not going to let her go home by herself. She nodded her head in acquiescence and even allowed him to hold her by the arm as they said goodbye to Carrie, walked down the stairs and, leaving the building, stepped out on to the pavement.

For Marta, who had been brought up in a small city, there were aspects of Manhattan that she still found astonishing. One was its nocturnal life. Other cities wound down after midnight, but for some New York residents it was the hour at which life really began. She and Casmir had to avoid an assortment of pedestrians—an old woman with a shopping cart, a pair of young lovers, two workmen carrying paint and a ladder. A taxi's horn blared as it swept around the corner followed by half-a-dozen other protesting cars; the sound of a tube train rumbled beneath the pavement. The city always had a roar to it, even at night; the noise muted and subdued but still evidence of busy life, of people coming and going, of a rush and bustle that was uniquely its own.

'You do not talk about yourself,' Casmir said as they began to walk.

Startled, Marta glanced up at him, noting the way the streetlights caught the slanted angle of his cheekbones and turned his hair into a lustrous bronze. 'I'm not very interesting,' she said.

'I do not think you are so humble,' he countered. 'You dance with a certain touch of arrogance.'

'I do!'

'You do not know this?'

Marta shook her head.

'It raised you above the corps, that edge of competence, that knowledge that you were better.'

'But I never thought that!' Marta objected. 'All I was trying to do was dance again after the accident.'

'Yes, the accident. I wonder about the accident.'

'I won't talk about it,' she said quickly.

'It is too painful?'

'Do you talk about your wife?' she countered.

He stopped her for a second, his hand tightening on her arm, and looked down into her eyes which were dark pools under the dim lights. 'You have bite, Marta. I did not know that.'

She was contrite; she had not meant to hurt him and had only lashed out to protect herself. She spent far too much time thinking about the past to want to discuss it with anyone. 'I'm sorry,' she said, 'but it's one of those verboten topics in my life.'

'You love your husband?'

'Yes.'

'He wasn't a dancer.'

'No, he was a bank manager.'

Casmir adroitly led them past an arguing couple who were standing in the middle of the pavement. 'It is unusual for dancers to marry outside of the ballet.'

'Your wife wasn't a ballerina, was she?'

'No, but she was part of the dance world; she was . . . how do you say?—savvy about ballet. She understood what it means.'

'Blaine understood, too,' Marta said softly. 'He knew what it meant to me. That made him special.'

Casmir glanced down at her. 'So no other man can match up to this Blaine, then? He occupies all of your heart?'

That wasn't true anymore, and Marta could not be sure that it had ever been true. Dancing had occupied her heart, not Blaine; but she had felt strongly about him, and she tried to express this to Casmir. 'He was an important part of my life,' she said, 'but he isn't here anymore and I've had to learn to live without him.'

'So you dance and dance and dance.'

Marta smiled at him, liking the way he had instinctively understood her. She had only known the public Casmir; a man of exuberance, large appetites and outrageous exaggeration. The private man was hidden, yet she thought she had caught a glimpse of an unexpected sensitivity. 'Yes,' she said.

'This feeling too I know,' Casmir said, throwing his arm in a wide and dramatic gesture towards the dark reaches of the night sky. 'I learn this after Bonnie is dead—that all is left is to dance. When I am on stage, when the eyes of the audience are upon me, there is no room in me for anything beyond the music and the motions. Perhaps, because the ballet is timeless. I do not know.'

There was a short silence as they walked, their legs moving in a matching rhythm, and then Marta asked a question that his confession had evoked. 'Had you been married for long?'

'Six months,' he said, his voice sombre. 'Not so long, but very, very intense. You know what I mean?'

'I don't know,' Marta confessed. 'Blaine and I had a different kind of relationship. We had known one another for years. Marriage for us was simply an extension of what had gone on before. We were ... comfortable together.'

'So, Marta the mysterious, you do not really know of love.'

She pulled her arm away from him. 'That's not true,' she objected. 'I loved him.'

Casmir shook his head. 'Love is not comfortable.'

They had turned the corner and had walked up to the front door of Marta's apartment building. They now stood beneath the awning that stretched out over the sidewalk. 'Thank you for escorting me,' she said in a formal tone. Marta hadn't liked the turn of the conversation, the talk of love making her uneasy. While they had discussed their marriages and their reactions to the deaths of their spouses, she had felt on familiar ground with Casmir; they had been fellow sufferers, but an analysis of the validity of her feelings towards Blaine struck Marta as dangerous. Casmir had, quite obviously, had a different experience of love, and she didn't want him to think that she required teaching in its variations. The rumours of his many affairs came back to her in full force, and she was wary that his talk of love was one of the ways in which he began a seduction. 'It's been a lovely evening,' she added, trying to turn away.

But Casmir was not about to let her go so easily. He blocked her way into the building, and he was scrutinising her in a curious fashion. '*Lapushka*,' he began, his voice serious, 'you have many previous lives. I can see it in your eyes.'

'I really don't believe in reincarnation,' Marta said. 'I don't believe that people die and are born again.'

He reached out and pulled a tendril of hair away from her mouth where a breeze had carried it. 'I do not mean other lifetimes; I talk about this one. You have so much melancholy, but I think perhaps you were different once. This Marta I know, she didn't exist before. Is that right?'

Marta pulled back from his hand. The gentleness of his gesture, the kindness of it, had shaken her more than she would have suspected was possible. It had been a long time since a man had touched her in such a soft and tender manner. 'Everyone passes through stages,' she said with an attempt to be crisp and pragmatic. 'No one remains the same.'

'But there is something missing in you. Tonight, for example, I see you laugh for the first time, and I think that perhaps there is a little part of Marta that disappeared when her husband died, when she was in that terrible accident.'

'Casmir, there's no point in. . . .'

'And you are very beautiful, you know.'

She shook her head. 'I'm not beautiful at all.'

'I do not talk about noses and chins,' he said. 'I talk about silence and sadness. I think of you as river, *milaya*; beautiful, flowing river so quiet in its banks, waiting . . .' She was mesmerised by the poetry of his words, the lilting Russian accent, the feel of his hand. He had cupped her chin and was lifting her face towards his so that all she could see was the darkness of his eyes, the light from the doorlamps turning his lashes into golden arcs. '. . . waiting to come alive again.'

'No. . . .'

'Yes.'

His mouth was so warm and soft, Marta found herself thinking with surprise, as his head bent over hers and she parted her mouth slightly in response to that pleasurable warmth. His lips moved on hers, gently and without any particular persistence, as if he too were savouring the sensations of the kiss, while his thumb made gentle circles on the hollow of her throat, the other hand caressing the line of her back and coming to rest on her waist. The kiss was exploratory, unthreatening, and almost tentative, until his tongue licked the corner of her mouth, and Marta felt the blood within her begin to surge, moving in the slow, heavy beat of desire. She had not felt anything like it in a long time, nor the sudden weakness in her legs nor the flush of heat that came into her cheeks. She had been attracted to Casmir physically, that she knew, but she had never guessed that it would be translated into such a sudden and intense longing merely at the touch of his mouth.

A vision of being in bed with him swamped her, their bodies entwined, an erotic melange of limbs and tongues and caresses. It took her breath away, causing Casmir to lift his head and look down at her with a smile. 'It is magic, is it not?'

She placed a hand against his chest so that he could not pull her close to him again. 'I don't want ... anything like this,' she said, her voice coming in a broken pattern as if she could not catch her breath. 'It isn't something that I'm prepared to do.'

'I know, *milaya*, I know.' With great tenderness, he touched her slightly opened mouth and then, lifting the finger to his own mouth, pressed his lips to its tip. 'Goodnight and sweet dreams.'

CHAPTER THREE

THE last two weeks before the tour was to begin had the company in a frenzy. Marta stood for hours before a mirror while the dresser, Mrs Martinelli, wandered in circles around her, muttering under her breath, her mouth bristling with pins. Marta was simply too tall to easily fit into Carrie's costumes and the alterations were many and frequent. *Sleeping Beauty* required tutus, and *Le Spectre de la Rose* a frilly, white dress with many petticoats and a cap. In *Le Corsaire* Marta would wear a slinky-looking harem outfit with her hair done up in a long braid with rhinestones and ribbons twined in its strands. That headpiece required new materials because Carrie had light hair and Marta's was dark, and the jewels and ribbons had to be of different colours for contrast.

The fittings for the tutus were the worst and, during them, Marta often wondered if audiences had any idea what lay behind the slender vision that they saw dancing on the stage. The skirt of a tutu had twelve layers of net held up by a wire hoop; the bodice was made of a heavy satin that was as tight as a second skin and was especially attached to the skirt so that the dancer could bend and stretch without ripping the fabric. Considering their age, the costumes were in better shape than Marta had expected, demonstrating the care that the wardrobe mistress and her assistant took to clean them after every performance when they were stained with perspiration and make-up, not only from the women's cosmetics, but also from the dark bases that the male ballet dancers wore on their faces.

But most of Marta's hours of preparation went into her point shoes, an irony when she considered how quickly they wore out. A new pair of shoes often had to be discarded after a twenty-minute ballet, their original shiny satin reduced to limp damp fabric, their shanks broken, the satin worn off the toe. It was Marta's habit before she had sewn on the ribbons and elastic on the shoes to dip their heels in alcohol to shrink the satin, spray hardner on the fabric for extra support, shave a bit of the leather off the bottom so they would not be slippery and to hammer the toes so that they wouldn't be so noisy. She often danced her way through ten pairs of point shoes a week, and while she shied away from thinking of how much those shoes cost the company, she did not hesitate to grumble and complain along with all the other dancers over the care they required. They all had a love–hate relationship with their shoes. Without them, there would be no ballet; inside them, it was often pure torture.

She did not see much of Casmir during this period except for rehearsals where they were worked so hard that there was no time for conversation. He treated her with the same casual kindness that he had bestowed on her before the kiss, and Marta came to the conclusion that the moment had been purely accidental, an intimacy inspired by the night, the walk and the meeting of minds that had occurred during their conversation. The kiss itself meant nothing really, and the fact that Casmir had never followed it up with anything more serious was a true indication of how he felt about her. They were companions and partners; they'd had life experiences in common. The kiss had been Casmir's way of showing affection; perhaps, Marta thought to herself with a touch of irony, she should be glad that he hadn't given her a bear hug instead. She'd seen Gregory turn almost white during the last time he'd been enveloped in Casmir's arms.

Still, there was no denying that she had enjoyed the physical caress in an unanticipated way, and she attributed this reaction to her solitary state, her loneliness, the sadness she felt within. It didn't take much, she thought wryly, to make her respond; a bit of gentleness, a touch of humour, the slightest hint of affection. It showed her just how vulnerable she really was despite all her efforts to ignore the existence of emotions and feelings. The night she had spent in a stranger's arms seeking anonymous caresses had moved her not at all; an innocent kiss in plain sight of New York's pedestrian traffic had made her tremble with desire. Did this mean that she was falling for Casmir with all his virility and sexual appeal? After long deliberation, Marta decided that this was not the case. What she had fallen for was his humanity and understanding. She needed friendship, she thought. Everyone did.

Marta spent the night before the tour was to begin packing and repacking her suitcase, agonising over choices of clothes and shoes and trying to make the hard decision over what had to be left behind. She had never gone on a company tour before and had received conflicting advice from the other dancers. Some seemed to only pack jeans and casual tops; others brought dressy clothes for the parties that would be thrown for the company. And there were already the hundred and one items she simply had to have: her dancing clothes, a sewing kit for emergencies, a first aid box, all the remedies she carried with which to treat her feet, a bag that bulged with combs, brushes and pins, her cosmetic case and an entire carry-all of low-calorie snacks.

This last was Marta's own private addition. She had visions of being so hungry when she travelled that she'd eat anything served to her; french fries, crisps, hamburgers slathered in ketchup and onions, coleslaw made with rich mayonnaise. Just the thought of it caused Marta's stomach to make an aching plea. Every dancer had his or her own personal food fetish; Carrie craved ice cream and Sandra had a passion for peanut butter and jelly. Marta was a junk food addict in her dreams while, in real life, she ate as sparingly as a bird, nibbling on sunflower seeds, carrots and celery. She weighed herself religiously every day, the slightest gain sending her into a panic. Marta had learned to put up with a lot as a dancer—painful feet, a strenuous schedule and a life that eliminated the social amenities that most people took for granted, but the hardest thing she had to bear was the constant dieting.

She had laid out three dresses on the bed and was studying each one, trying to decide which would wash without a wrinkle and look as fresh as a daisy after days of being crumpled in her suitcase, when Simone came into her bedroom and sat down in the chair beside the bed, wrapping her blue velvet robe around her. She had a way, Marta noticed, of looking as if she'd just stepped out of the pages of a fashion magazine no matter what time of day it was. Her nails were long and coral, her eye make-up was complete and she had not a pale-red hair out of place.

'It looks like you're leaving for a year instead of a month,' Simone said.

'There's too many decisions to make,' Marta said, 'and only one small suitcase.' She frowned at the dresses.

'I met Dr Block last night at the Gibson's house. He wanted to know how you were doing.'

'Fine,' Marta said.

Simone ignored her. 'He thought that being the prima ballerina on a tour might be a strain on your legs.'

'Dr Block never even thought I would dance again. I've proved him wrong already.'

Simone raised a drawn-in eyebrow. 'Heavens, Marta. You don't have to be so touchy. No one's trying to hold you back; we're merely concerned.'

Marta glanced at her in scepticism. Simone's concern had always been questionable. She could not be faulted in doing her duty by Marta; she had rushed to Syracuse after the accident and stayed by Marta's bedside, insisting that only the best surgeons and orthopaedist would do, but beyond that her sympathy seemed false and contrived. Once Marta was in New York, she was left to the care of a physiotherapist and the Cole's cook who fussed over her initial lack of appetite, feeding her custards and cakes designed to entice even the most reluctant eater. No, Marta thought, her mother had never been one to worry, and she wasn't about to tell her that, yes, her legs did bother her and that she prayed nightly that they wouldn't get any worse. Right now, the pain was bearable; an occasional shooting dart in one thigh, an ache behind the knee in the other leg. But Marta knew that the stress of ballet could intensify her problems; Dr Block had been quite emphatic about that. He hadn't wanted her to dance in the first place.

'If they start bothering,' Marta lied, 'I'll stop dancing.'

'Well, it would be a shame to cripple yourself,' Simone answered. 'There's so many other things to do in life besides dancing.'

Marta didn't bother to answer. Her philosophy of life and her mother's were so at odds that they might as well have inhabited separate planets. Simone flitted from one thing to another while Marta had a perseverance that verged on bull-headedness. She had gone into ballet at an early age and with determination, her focus never veering for one second from the goal of becoming a ballerina. Simone, on the other hand, was more hedonistic, enjoying the luxuries of life and its myriad pleasures. While she did not scorn Marta's career, she was totally mystified by the sacrifices that her daughter was willing to make. Sweat and pain were an anathema to Simone; she preferred elegant lounging, designer clothes and *haute cuisine*.

If pressed to talk about her relationship to Simone, Marta was apt to shrug and say that they'd never really been mother and daughter and could never be considered friends. Simone was proud of her, she would go on to explain, but that's as far as the emotions went. Basically, she'd been brought up by a housekeeper, ballet teachers and neighbours. Her father had been a remote figure, often away on business, and Simone had either accompanied him or taken her own pleasure trips. If asked whether this had upset her, Marta would give a small smile and shrug again. Whatever hurt had arisen from her relationship with her parents she had suppressed years earlier when she had decided that she wanted to be a dancer and focused all her energies on ballet. Now, when she and Simone were together, the atmosphere was cool, the conversation polite and the participants wary.

'Was there anything else?' Marta asked, placing her sewing kit on top of her jeans.

'I wondered if you'd planned to get in touch with Blaine's parents when the company stops in Syracuse.'

Slowly Marta straightened up. 'I wasn't sure. . . .'

'Peggy says you don't write to them at all. She's quite upset about it.'

Marta turned away towards the wardrobe so that Simone could not see her face. 'I should have answered her last letter, but I was so involved that I. . . .'

'As far as I can see, you haven't opened her letters or returned her phone calls,' Simone said coldly. 'And considering the time she spent with you and the fact that she considered you almost a daughter, I hardly think it was right to cut off all communication after Blaine's death.'

Marta blindly pulled a skirt off a hanger, not even knowing which one it was. 'Do you talk to her often?'

'We write; I thought you knew that.'

Marta's voice was muffled in the wardrobe. 'No.'

'Whatever your personal reluctance to see the Morrison's again, I think it would be impolite and highly inconsiderate if you don't contact them when you're in Syracuse. They're going to know you're in town; the papers will be full of publicity.'

Marta pressed her face against the cool sleeve of a silk blouse. 'I will,' she said.

'Marta, I can't hear a word you're saying.'

'I will,' she said in a louder voice. 'I'll call them. I promise.'

'Fine,' Simone said, standing up. 'I think you should.'

When Simone had closed the door behind her, Marta finally turned away from the wardrobe and put her hand up to her face, feeling the dampness of tears on her cheeks. She was thankful that Simone had no real curiosity about her and had not pressed for the reason why she hadn't written to Peggy and Dave Morrison in the last two years. Marta did not like to lie, but she would have been forced to. The truth was so unbearable that it was something she hid even from herself when she could. And the thought of facing the Morrison's, knowing what she did, was almost too painful to contemplate.

Peggy had, in some ways, been the mother Marta had never had. She was the next-door neighbour who Marta had visited after school when there was no one in her house but the maid, who had bestowed on her cakes, hugs and sympathy and who had been the most excited when Marta's career had blossomed. Peggy had not a mean bone in her body; Marta wasn't the only neighbourhood child who had been the beneficiary of her mothering and concern. Many of the children from the surrounding houses gathered at the Morrison house where the ambiance was warm, casual and designed for children. There were five Morrison boys, each two years apart and almost inseparable. They all looked as if they'd been cut out by the same biscuit-cutter; they were all tall, skinny, snub-nosed and freckled. The only difference had been in hair colour, which ranged from almost black to blond. Blaine, one of the middle sons, had received light-brown hair, the family's green eyes and the least amount of freckles.

As a single child and a lonely one at that, Marta had been fascinated and thrilled by what went on at the Morrison's. The house was always full of activity: the boys coming and going with their friends; a radio playing in one room, a stereo in another; good smells emanating from the kitchen, a room that was never empty because someone in the household was always hungry; and Peggy presiding over it all with serenity and smiles. She was a large woman, big-boned and fleshy, who tended to dress in bibbed overalls and her husband's T-shirts. She sculpted in the odd moments when she wasn't arbitrating over a quarrel, picking up toys, socks and shoes or cooking to feed her family, and Marta had spent many hours in Peggy's studio watching her work and admiring the figures that were created by those strong fingers. Dave Morrison was an investment counsellor who'd made a killing in the stock market and was semi-retired even when Marta was a child. He was the kind of man who liked to build things—tree-houses, pogo sticks, wooden racing cars that little boys could pedal up and down the sidewalk.

It hurt Marta even to think about them and remember the love and care they had given her. They'd been indulgent when she and Blaine had gone steady with adolescent fervour, and thrilled when that teenage infatuation had developed into a relationship far stronger and deeper. They had never questioned Marta's career plans or worried that she wouldn't have the time to lavish devotion on their son. Everyone in the Morrison family had felt that Marta's triumphs were their own. She would never forget their faces staring up at her from the audience during her performances with the Syracuse Dance Company. They formed one of the loudest cheering squads that the company had ever known, and the Director had wryly referred to them after one particularly enthusiastic call for ovations and encores as 'Marta's Mob'.

The Morrisons had been wonderful to her, and Marta's guilt at not keeping in touch with them was deep and painful. Not writing to them or phoning them made Marta seem callous, cold-hearted, and very ungrateful, but she was none of these things. She had yearned to talk to Peggy and Dave after Blaine's death; she would have given anything to be part of their mourning and wrapped up in their sympathy and love once again. But she had fled from Syracuse, from them, from the memories of Blaine, and it wasn't only her shattered dreams that had made her go. Marta had been unable to face the Morrisons, knowing what she did: that *she* had been responsible for the accident, that if it hadn't been for her, the car would not have crashed and Blaine would still be alive; smiling the lazy smile that made the skin crinkle around his eyes and rubbing his head in a characteristic gesture that tousled his hair and made it fall forward on his forehead in an attractive, boyish curl.

The first of a series of random accidents that were to plague the company throughout the tour happened on the plane as the dancers were boarding. A suitcase fell out of an overhead compartment on to the shoulder of one of the male dancers who insisted that he wasn't hurt in the least, but who had to be sent back to New York when they arrived in Hartford, where he was taken to a hospital, X-rayed and diagnosed as having a cracked shoulder blade. Like many creative people, dancers were suspicious and there was a certain glumness in the air as they all took their seats and the plane took off.

Sandra, who was seated next to Marta, commented as she put on her safety belt, 'I wonder if it's an omen.'

'I left my crystal ball at home,' Marta replied, resting her head against the seat and closing her eyes. She had had a bad night's sleep, thinking about the Morrisons and she was hoping to nap on the plane.

'Falling suitcases could lead to turned ankles, broken bones, crashing planes . . .' she took a deep breath and Marta completed the list for her, '. . . lost scenery, missing costumes, and bored audiences.'

'Well, you must admit it isn't the most auspicious beginning. One hopes to be in the middle of a tour before the disasters begin to strike.'

Marta opened her eyes. 'You mean it happens a lot?'

Sandra groaned. 'You have no idea. I'd suggest heart-felt prayer.'

They stopped talking for a moment as the stewardess gave them emergency instructions, and then Sandra said casually, 'Did you notice who's seated next to Casmir?'

'Cynthia, no doubt.'

'Mmmm—I wonder what's happening there. I heard about a reconciliation but it's hard to say. You know what gossip is like.'

'I do—that's why I don't indulge in it.'

'And you're one of the most interesting topics.'

Marta gave Sandra a startled glance. 'I am?'

'No men, no vices, a career that took off like a helium balloon—what do you think?'

'Are you suggesting that people think I . . . slept my way into being Casmir's partner?' Marta asked, her eyes going wide with anger.

'Hold your horses and don't get your water hot,' Sandra said soothingly. 'No one's actually suggested a thing.'

Marta was unappeased. 'Ballet dancers have such dirty minds.'

'It's a universal condition,' Sandra said. 'And it goes on in every profession I can think of. My sister works for a bank and if you think that's a bastion of respectability, then think again.'

'I'm not a prude,' Marta said, 'but I really wish that people would concentrate on their own lives rather than speculating about others.'

Sandra made an airy gesture in the air with her hand. 'Life would be too boring,' she drawled.

'I don't think it's boring.'

'You're either a saint,' Sandra said with a smile, 'or your own life is so satisfying that you don't have time to think about anyone else.'

Marta made a grimace. 'Well, I've never been a saint and as for my life. . . .' Her voice trailed off as if there wasn't anything in her private life worth mentioning.

But Sandra wasn't so easily put off. 'Did your husband mind that you were a dancer?'

The question was so direct and unexpected that Marta forgot to be evasive. 'No, he didn't,' she said.

'Lucky you.'

Despite the casual tone of Sandra's voice, there was something brittle in it that caused Marta to sit up and take notice. It occurred to her for the first time that, despite the other dancer's tendency to gossip, Sandra was exceedingly close-mouthed about herself, and Marta had no idea what she did beyond the hours that she spent at the studio or in performance. She watched Sandra pick up a magazine and begin to leaf through it and debated asking the other woman what was the matter. She didn't like people probing into her life and, in turn, she respected the privacy of others, but Sandra was so obviously unhappy that Marta's sympathies were aroused. Still, she might not have said anything if Sandra hadn't taken that moment to blink as if she were trying to hold back tears.

'Sandra, I don't mean to pry, but is there anything wrong?' Marta asked gently.

The other woman gave her a startled glance. 'It's that obvious? God, I must be a walking advertisement for depression and neuroses.' She tried to laugh it off and then, to the consternation of both of them, proceeded to burst into tears.

'Sandra!'

'Oh, hell, this is so embarrassing,' Sandra sniffed and grabbed a tissue from her purse. 'Pardon the waterworks. I tend to run dry eventually.'

'I didn't mean to upset you.'

Sandra blew her nose. 'It isn't you; it's the love of my life who walked out about two months ago and hasn't returned.' She reached down and, pulling a compact from her purse, opened it. 'There goes my mascara,' she added with a half-sob, half-laugh. 'Someone should invent real tear-proof cosmetics, don't you think? They'd make an easy million.'

Marta ignored Sandra's obvious attempt to divert the conversation. 'I didn't know you were living with someone.'

'I didn't broadcast it. I . . . well, I guess I believed that it was a bluff, his walking out like that without a word or a hint.' She gave an unhappy shrug of her shoulders. 'I knew things weren't going well, but I truly thought he'd show up again, and I'd go home thinking he'd be waiting for me at the apartment or standing outside the stage door the way he used to. I thought . . . oh, there's no point in talking about what I thought, because it's obvious he doesn't have any intention of coming back.'

'Who was it?' Marta asked. 'Another dancer?'

'No, someone outside ballet. That was part of the problem; he couldn't handle my lifestyle. At first he was thrilled by the glamour of it all, but after a while he got bored because I wasn't home in the evenings, or if I was, I was too tired to go out. It's really a rotten life, you know.'

'Is there any chance of calling him, of talking it out. . . .'

Sandra shook her head and blew her nose again. 'I couldn't crawl that way, and I know what he's like. He'd despise me for it. Besides, I suspect that he's got another woman already. He isn't the type of man who can live without women and . . . well, I really don't want to know about it. That's the reason why I haven't tried to see him again. I don't want to be confronted with the fact that he's sleeping with someone else.' She gave Marta a mournful smile. 'There are really times when ignorance is bliss, aren't there?'

Marta knew precisely what Sandra meant, although she did not actually say so. She spent the rest of the plane ride offering sympathy and a willing ear while Sandra dissected her old boyfriend with the bitterness of a woman scorned. But after the discussion was over, and they had landed in Hartford, the echoes of Sandra's earlier statement came back to haunt her. Ignorance *was* bliss, and Marta knew she would have been much happier if the evidence of Casmir's and Cynthia's love affair had not been quite so obvious. Not that she was in love with Casmir herself or wanted to be involved with him but, for some reason, she did not like the constant reminders that they were a couple. The sight of Cynthia hanging on Casmir's arm or smiling up into his eyes or talking to him intensely were sights she had been spared at the studio. Now that the company was on tour and the dancers thrown together in the confines of an aeroplane or hotel lobby, relationships were cast into sharp relief.

Marta's contact with Cynthia had been minimal during rehearsals. Their paths rarely crossed and when they did she had received an impression of a pixiesh face, sharp green eyes and a cool demeanour. She was well aware that the other dancer was jealous; feelings like that were common in ballet companies and Marta had once been just as consumed with ambition and envy. On the few occasions they met she and Cynthia had chatted pleasantly and then gone their separate ways. Out of sight was out of mind, and Marta rarely thought about the other dancer when she was not present, but having her constantly in view and quite publicly on display as Casmir's lover came as something of a shock.

During the next few days Marta tried studiously to avoid being near them or within hearing distance of their conversations, but luck was not always with her. On the third night of the tour she was walking down the hotel corridor towards her room when she passed by the door of Casmir's and heard Cynthia laughing inside. The laugh seemed to echo in her head all night, and she slept uneasily, the crazy quilt of her dreams stitched with images of Casmir's blond head, Cynthia's hazel eyes, limbs twisted and entwined. When Marta woke the next morning and faced her tired visage in the mirror, she confronted the fact that she still had a strong and undeniable physical attraction to Casmir.

She had thought to dismiss it; she had thought it would be easy to forget or ignore, and she had partially succeeded during rehearsals. But the knowledge that Casmir was sleeping with another woman just yards away from her own bedroom had provoked her own sexual longings, drawn them out and brought them to the forefront of her conscious mind.

As she brushed out the tangles in her black hair and pulled it up tightly in a dancer's chignon, Marta knew that none of her feelings must show and that she must learn either to live with them or successfully suppress them. Casmir had meant nothing by the kiss he had bestowed on her with such careless and gallant tenderness. His heart had been elsewhere; his thoughts directed towards another woman who clearly satisfied him and made him happy. She had seen him smile down at Cynthia, and it was the smile of a man who knew a woman intimately and liked what he knew. How ironic it was, Marta thought, as she stared into her own black-fringed, blue eyes, that she was where Cynthia wanted to be—dancing in Casmir's arms, while Cynthia was where *she* wanted to be—held in Casmir's arms: caressed, touched and loved with all the exuberance of his great Russian heart.

On the fifth and last night of their stay in Hartford, a sudden stabbing pain in her left leg during the finale of *Sleeping Beauty* caused Marta to miss a step and fall into Casmir's arms, a move he covered up quite adroitly by lifting her slightly and dipping his own body in time with the music. She completed the final steps without any problem, and the troupe received a standing ovation at the end, each dancer stepping forward to take his or her bow and Marta receiving an armful of fragrant roses as she curtsied. As the curtain closed for the last time the dancers exchanged weary smiles and some of them limped into the wings, their on-stage personas—the smiles, the rigid backs, the regal tilt of head—disappearing completely now that they were no longer on view.

There were agonised moans backstage as the dancers filed into the dressing-rooms and the inevitable analysis began.

'It wasn't my night. Did you see the way I missed the bourrée . . .?'

'My feet feel terrible. This is the last time I'm going to wear this brand of point shoe. I told Gregory. . . .'

'Did anyone see me bump Lonnie? What a disaster!'

Marta walked past the closed door to the dressing-room for the corps, but she could easily imagine what it's interior was like. Dancers would be sinking down on the chairs, pulling their hair out of tight buns, stripping off their eyelashes, easing throbbing feet out of their shoes. The room would look as if a storm had raged through: the floor scattered with tights, leotards, point shoes, empty cans of soda and balls of lamb's wool floating around like tumbleweeds. The dressing tables would be filled with opened jars of make-up, tubes, brushes, hairpins, brushes and crumpled tissues. Marta could hear the sounds of voices, laughter and groans as she passed, and she knew how the dancers were rehashing each step and every nuance of movement that had occurred that night. This was what they lived and trained for so long and so arduously— the scant hour that they spent on the stage, the illusion that they created for the audience, and that brief moment when they too could believe that they were different than other mortals; ethereal and graceful creatures that defied gravity and muscle and bone.

The irony was, Marta thought as she walked towards her own dressing-room, that dancers were as earthbound as anyone, but they hated to admit it. They fought normal body position and movement, often to the detriment of their own health. Her leg had given way, it was true, but she considered her own private pain as no different from the normal aches and pains of dancing. There were plenty of performers who went on-stage every day with problem feet, knees and backs. The important thing was to be prepared for the pain, to exercise against it and to be aware that it might pounce at any minute.

She pushed open the door to her dressing-room and began to unpin the rhinestone tiara from her hair as she walked in.

'I have been waiting for you.'

Casmir was leaning back on the chair by her make-up table, his arms crossed over his bare chest. He'd had a chance, Marta saw, to wash. His blond hair was damp and curling over his forehead; she could see beads of water resting on the expanse of his shoulders and glinting in the golden hair on his torso that angled down over his muscled abdomen to a line descending into the top of his tights. She had an urge to lean forward and touch one droplet that was slowly working its way down the column of his neck to the deep indentation of his throat, but she gripped her hands at her sides and gave him a wary smile.

'Sorry about missing that step,' she said. 'I don't know what happened.'

'It is not like you to do that,' he said.

'No,' Marta agreed, putting the tiara on the dressing table. 'I'm sorry.'

He watched her for a moment as she pulled the pins out of her hair, letting its full length swing to her shoulders, creating a dark halo around her face. Not even the theatrical make-up—the lines drawn around her eyes and the rouge on her cheeks—could hide the pallor of her skin or the mauve shadows under her eyes.

'You look tired,' he said.

Marta rubbed her head where the pins had pressed into her scalp. 'I'm not used to being on tour and sleeping in strange beds. I'm going to have to learn to adjust.'

'You danced differently tonight.'

She gave him a wide-eyed glance. 'I did?'

'You did not notice?' The blue eyes impaled her as if she were a butterfly pinned to a board.

In order that Casmir could not see her face, Marta

sat down on the couch and, leaning forward, began to unknot the ribbons of her point shoes. 'No.'

'We got a standing ovation for it.'

She unwound the ribbons and rubbed her ankles. 'Some nights are better than others, I guess.'

'No, Marta, some nights dancers relate to one another differently.'

She could not answer him; she could not begin to explain what her physical attraction to him meant in terms of her dancing. She had been aware of him that night in a way she'd never been aware of him before. She'd been conscious every moment of his presence; his body, his wide hands on her waist, the arms that lifted her, the bent leg that supported her in the *attitude croise*, the taut muscle of his thigh against her hip. At one point they had both stood in opposing wings, waiting for the music to sound that would send them leaping out at one another, and she had seen him shake his arms and shoulders in preparation for the moment when all her weight would land on him. For some reason that gesture had made her heart skip a beat as if, instead of readying himself for her on-stage leap, he were readying himself for some private and intimate embrace.

'I notice things, *milaya*,' he went on. 'I notice that you are a different Aurora tonight.'

'I felt the story more,' she said carefully.

'Your heart beat beneath my hands. I could feel it shaking your chest whenever I touch you.'

Marta's defence was flattery. She knew the kind of man Casmir was; she knew how large an ego he had. 'It was you,' she said, batting her eyes at him. 'Who can resist?'

He was on his feet in a second, standing over her and glaring down at her in a manner so ferocious that Marta looked up in fright, one point shoe half off. 'Do not flirt with me, Marta. I do not want that from you.'

She had never seen him so angry; his nostrils flared in fury, the skin around his nose and tight-lipped mouth white. His blue eyes had darkened and his hands were clenched at his side as if they were resisting an urge to take her by the throat and throttle her. Marta could see a pulse throbbing in the side of his neck, the blue vein running over one broad shoulder and then disappearing until it emerged on his upper arm where the bicep swelled with the strength of his clenched grip. Every muscle of his chest was in sharp definition, and Marta thought she could hear his heart pounding against his ribs. Casmir was magnificent in his rage; he was altogether the most magnificent man and suddenly the most terrifying man she had ever seen.

Unconsciously her hand rose to her throat. 'I don't really want to flirt with you either,' she said.

'I can get that from any woman,' he said.

'Yes, I know.'

'But you are not any woman. You are my partner.'

But she couldn't tell him the truth; she just couldn't come out and say what she had felt in his arms. 'I don't know why I danced that way. You just ... seemed special tonight.'

He stared down at her for a moment, watching her, appraising her and finally judging her. 'All right, *lyubimaya*. I accept that.' He reached down and ran one finger along the line of her cheek. 'You too are special. I want you to know that—there are times I dance just for you.'

And with that he was gone, while Marta stared after him, her hand moving up to her cheek where his finger had caressed her and left a trail of warmth. Casmir had an awesome power over her, she discovered, to evoke the most intense sensations; to make her breath catch in her throat, to make her heart race in a sudden burst of speed, to make a trembling begin deep within her. It was terrible that a man was able to do this simply by touching her cheek, but he did. Unfortunately, he did.

CHAPTER FOUR

In Providence disaster took several forms. The first was the loss of Casmir's costume for *Le Spectre de la Rose*. It took several frantic phone calls to discover that the costume had been left behind in Hartford when the wardrobe mistress had packed and was found, not in Casmir's dressing-room, but backstage behind a prop. All concerned with the costume scatched their heads over this last bit of information, and the wardrobe assistant went around looking exceedingly morose as if she were to blame, although she kept assuring anyone she came up to that she had never even seen the costum, much less misplaced it. When it was finally learned that there was not a chance in heaven or hell of getting that costume to Providence in time for the performance that night, the tension mounted. More frantic phone calls to dance shops elicited a leotard and tights in rose and one hundred squares of variously shaded pink felt. Not less than two hours before the curtain was to open, everyone in the company who could wield a needle and thread were working on the costume—with Casmir already in it.

He stood in the centre of his dressing-room while some dancers cut out petals from the felt and others sewed them on to the leotard, the wardrobe mistress giving out terse instructions. Although the original costume had been a work of art, with a matching cap, an ensemble that gave him the look of a creature that has indeed come out of an unfurled rose, this one promised to be something less than artistic, a fact that he commented on frequently whenever he caught sight of himself in the mirror. His head was to be bare, and the petals were being sewn along the chest, back and shoulders of the leotard in overlapping rows. Marta, who was pinning petals on to his chest, prayed that he'd resemble something floral, but it was obvious that Casmir was convinced he'd be ridiculous.

'This gives the appearance of a half-plucked chicken,' he said morosely.

'Think flowers,' Cynthia said. She was sewing a pink petal on to his shoulder.

'Think roses and thorns,' someone else suggested.

Sandra was sitting on the floor with her legs crossed, cutting out petals. 'Think what we can become when we get too old to dance—tailors.'

'I don't plan to get too old,' Cynthia said. 'I'm going to dance forever!'

'Ah—the younger they are, the harder they'll fall,' Sandra said. 'Nobody dances forever.'

But Cynthia was not to be deterred. 'When will you stop dancing, Casmir?' she asked.

'Until I drop,' he said, 'or until the audience hisses me off the stage.'

'I can't imagine not dancing,' she said, as she plied a needle through another petal.

'Oh, I can,' Sandra said tartly. 'I can easily imagine living an ordinary life, getting up at a regular hour in the morning, going to bed at a decent hour at night and having a normal social life.'

'But what would you *do*?' another dancer asked.

'I'd work.'

'Where?'

Sandra cut out another petal. 'Anywhere—an office, a school, the grocery store. I don't know. What I'd want is continuity; nine to five every day with weekends off and dinner at six.'

'Imagine no rehearsals,' someone else added.

'And no point shoes,' another dancer threw in.

It was easy for them, Marta thought to herself as she picked up a petal and a pin, to think about a life without dance, but none of them had actually experienced one. She knew how empty it was, and how the hours and days could drag. In some ways, dancing was like an addictive drug—a way of getting a high and a thrill beyond anything else imaginable. When she was up on the stage, and thousands of eyes spoke only to her, it was then that Marta knew she was most alive.

'Ouch!'

Marta looked up into Casmir's frowning blue eyes. 'I'm sorry,' she said. 'Did I prick you?'

'I am human pincushion,' Casmir said gloomily.

'Poor Casmir,' Cynthia said soothingly as she eyed Marta over Casmir's shoulder. 'It's only for one night and we'll have Sunday to recuperate.'

Marta was very quick to catch the 'we' that Cynthia had let drop in such a casual tone, and also to note the proprietary look in those hazel eyes. The other dancer was diminutive but strong-willed, a characteristic that came out in the glance that she was giving Marta and in the tiny hand she had placed on Casmir's broad shoulder. The message was loud and clear, the territory carefully mapped the boundaries strongly marked, and Marta couldn't help wondering how Casmir handled that possessive jealousy. Perhaps he wanted it; perhaps he was flattered by the way Cynthia felt about him. Marta couldn't be sure because he had turned slightly, taken Cynthia's hand in his and was raising it to his lips, while giving her a flirtatious glance from between gold-tipped lashes.

'Ah,' he said, 'the recuperation. That is the best part, is it not?'

Cynthia did not answer but gave his bent head a small, knowing smile that caused Marta to inwardly cringe. It was so blatantly sexual and such an overt proclamation of their status as lovers that she backed away from it and sat down beside Sandra who was still busily cutting out petals.

'Pink or red?' she asked in as light a tone as she could manage.

'Red,' Sandra said with a wicked grin. 'We're going to find out if he's blue-blooded or not—from the pinpricks.'

It was to go down in the annals of The Manhattan Ballet Company as 'the night Casmir lost his petals', and Marta was always to wonder if the audience thought that the falling foliage was part of the romanticism of the ballet, because their enthusiasm was not deterred by the pieces of fluttering felt that adorned the stage. They applauded wildly afterwards while she and Casmir bowed and curtsied, their hands gripped together, both thankful that neither had tripped or slipped on the bits of fabric on the stage floor. If it had got bad enough she was sure Gregory would have stopped the music and sent a stagehand out to gather up the litter. She had occasionally caught sight of those watching in the wings, their expressions indicating either suppressed hilarity or horror, and she'd give them a dreamy smile in keeping with her role, while Casmir would whisper in her ear, 'I am shedding, goddamn.'

The company was thrown a party that night by the local theatre guild, and Marta enjoyed the feeling of glamour it gave her to be wined, dined and fêted by locals who were thrilled to have a New York company performing in their town. The spread of food was wonderful; huge salads, roast beef, shellfish and champagne, and everyone in the company ate and drank as if there were no tomorrow. Marta made conversation with several members of the audience and heard stories of ballets seen once and dreamed about, of daughters who wanted to become dancers, of woman who had always wished that they could dance. The awe she was held in made her realise how the rest of the world held dancers apart—as if they were special, as if they were touched by magic, as if they were gods and goddesses with talents no one else could possess.

It was, she was to think later in the small hours of the morning when they had all gone back to the hotel, rather ironic for the public to feel that dancers were any different from anyone else, and she wondered

how awe-struck their adoring public would have
remained if they could hear the sounds coming out of
Casmir's room.

She had already gone to bed and was close to sleep
when she first became aware of voices coming through
the wall in a discussion that had been turned up to a
high volume. One voice was male and the other female,
but the words were indistinguishable. Then the
throwing had started, or at least that's how Marta
diagnosed the thuds that made the wall between the two
rooms shudder. When one thud resulted in a loud
crash, like glass breaking, she got out of bed and pulled
on her bathrobe. She opened her door, peered in both
directions down the quiet corridor and wondered if the
noise had been a figment of her own imagination.

Then Cynthia's voice came through the door panel.
'I've never met anyone so inconsiderate, so thoughtless,
so . . .'

Casmir's voice was a deep mumble.

'. . . so arrogant or self-centred!' Another crash. 'And
if you think I'm going to keep coming back for more,
then you had better think again. I'm not a toy to be
discarded when it's used. I have feelings, too!'

Another male rumble.

'You're sorry!? Sorry? Is that the only thing you can
say?' Cynthia's voice was rising in pitch to the point
that Marta winced. A door down the corridor opened
and another dancer peered out. When she caught sight
of Marta, she gave her a questioning glance which
Marta returned with a shrug that expressed confusion
and ignorance. The dancer gave her a small wave and
closed her door.

'Well, I'm sorry too,' Cynthia raged on. 'Sorry for
the time I wasted on you, sorry for thinking that you
were decent and caring and kind. Frankly,' and the
door to Casmir's room was flung open, 'I hate you and
I want you to know it!'

Cynthia exited in a flurry of blue nightgown and
robe, her long red hair rippling down her back like a

flame. Marta couldn't help thinking how beautiful Cynthia was. Anger transformed her, heightening the colour of her usually pale complexion and turning her hazel eyes into glittering emeralds. She barely acknowledged Marta's presence as she swept past her down the hall, her hands gripped at her sides, her jaw clenched with fury. Marta stood uncertainly in the corridor for a few more minutes and then, walking to the opened door of Casmir's room, peered inside. She couldn't see anyone, but she heard the clinking of a glass.

'Casmir?'

'"Hell hath no fury like a woman scorned,"' a voice quoted as she closed the door behind her and stepped further into the room. It was lit by only one light on the bedside table which caught the gleam of the vodka bottle, the golden glint of Casmir's hair and the diamond-like glitter of broken glass that was strewn in front of the dressing table. He was lying on his back across the still-made double bed, dressed only in the bottom half of his pyjamas, a cream colour that matched the bedspread. His bare torso, bronzed and rugged, was propped up against several pillows, and his face looked weary, his hair tumbling on his forehead as if he had run his fingers through its strands in tired exasperation. In one hand he held a glass with the clear liquid of vodka sloshing around inside. 'Aha,' he went on, 'an angel in disguise,' and raising his glass to her, added, 'cheers.'

For a second, Marta stood there, the hem of her white robe brushing against her bare toes, and then she adroitly sidestepped the bits of broken glass and, tucking her robe more tightly around her, walked up to the chair that stood near the bed. She had no idea if Casmir wanted or needed company, and she wasn't sure that she had any desire to be the recipient of his confidences. On the other hand, she'd heard stories about the way he could put away a bottle of vodka, and she knew how detrimental drinking would be for his dancing. Gregory would be furious if he'd found that

Casmir had got himself stinking drunk, and they'd spend the next twenty-four hours trying to sober him up for the Sunday matinee.

But Marta was not exactly sure how she could stop him from drinking so she sat down in the chair and said, 'Cheers.'

'You wish a drink of good Russian vodka?' he asked.

There were, Marta realised suddenly, more than one way to skin a cat. 'Sure,' she said. 'Why not?'

'You are accustomed to drinking vodka?'

'Well, I've never. . . .'

'I will teach you,' he said. 'It is necessary to pay attention.' He got up off the bed and, going into the bathroom, came out again with another glass. 'The best way to think about vodka,' he went on in a conversational tone, 'is to think of it as menial.'

It took Marta a moment to comprehend. 'Medicinal,' she said.

'That's it,' he said, giving her a grin. 'You have the gift of words.'

She couldn't help smiling at him as he handed her a tumbler full of vodka. There was something so endearing about Casmir; a combination of muscular virility, the boyish tumble of blond hair on his broad forehead, the eloquent look in his blue eyes. He was, she thought as she watched him take a long swallow of his own drink, an uncomplicated man, one who wore his heart on his sleeve, every emotion visible and intense. This, of course, was part of his appeal, and Marta couldn't blame Cynthia for her infatuation. Each woman he came in contact with was convinced, deep inside, that if Casmir wanted her, then she would be bathed in the constant sunlight of his love; protected, cared for, desired and adored. And, in turn, he liked women; truly liked them. She had seen him listen attentively to ballerinas discuss everything from point shoes to tutus, from the state of their love lives to the length of their hair, and his interest didn't diminish his masculinity in the least. She had never met a man who was so completely male.

'Now, the important thing,' he said, sitting down on the edge of the bed, 'is to take a full swallow. The vodka, she doesn't have a taste, but when she reaches the inside of you, she will make herself known.'

Marta gave him a wary smile as she raised her glass in imitation of his. She had a feeling her insides were not going to be pleased to make the acquaintance of Casmir's vodka.

'Now, a big swallow.' Casmir lifted his glass and she watched with awe as he drank.

'I don't think. . . .' she began.

Casmir frowned at her as he put his glass down. 'You must drink,' he said.

Marta obediently took a sip, tried to keep her expression impassive as the vodka made its presence known, burning a fiery path down her oesophagus and right into her stomach, and prayed fervently that somebody somewhere would reward her for this sacrifice. She never drank, but her glass of vodka was one less glass that Casmir would drink.

'Good?' he asked.

Marta coughed a bit and then nodded. 'Great vodka.'

'The best,' Casmir said with satisfaction, leaning back against pillows and propping himself up on one elbow. 'The best Russian vodka. It will put hair on your chest.'

'Just what I needed,' she said dryly.

'So,' he said pouring himself another drink, 'we wake you up?'

'I never actually went to sleep.'

'I am sorry for this disturbance, but love affairs do not always end in neat packages.'

'It's over then?'

Casmir stretched, the planes of muscles in his chest moving, the depth of his ribcage revealed, the hollow of his abdomen accentuated as his arms reached above his head. Marta looked away from him to her glass and tried another sip of vodka, wanting the sting of it to take away the feelings that Casmir's body awoke in her.

'Over,' he echoed. 'It should have been over weeks ago, but I didn't have the heart to hurt her.'

'You seemed very close,' Marta ventured.

'She is so young,' he said. 'Ten years younger than I am and very naïve. She thinks I want to marry her if I make love to her. She cannot understand that my feelings for her do not extend that deeply.'

'A lot of women want to marry their lovers,' Marta said, thinking of Sandra.

'I wish for something casual, not for something permanent. I . . .' and he took another swig of vodka. 'I am lonely after Bonnie; I need a woman. You understand this?'

Marta's mouth had gone dry. 'Yes,' she whispered. 'Very well.'

Casmir sat up and looked at her. 'You have a man since your husband's death?'

Marta nodded and looked down into her glass, not wanting to talk about it, but too honest to conceal it.

'You live with him?'

'No, I . . . it was a very casual thing—just an encounter, really.'

'It made you happy?'

Marta looked up at him, her eyes dark with sad reminiscence. 'No, it had the opposite effect. I was very unhappy after it; it had been so shallow.'

'You know,' Casmir said, leaning back against the pillow again and studying the liquor in his glass, 'before I marry, I think of women as candy. I gobble them up, tasting the sweetness of each, before going on to the next. I love them all, but not one is enough for a meal, for a lifetime. And then I notice Bonnie. She is like me, a bit. She has many boyfriends, many lovers. She treats them all the same, but inside she has held a part of herself a . . . how do you say it?'

'Aloof?'

'Yes, she keeps separate from these affairs. Not one man touches her heart deeply. When I pursue her, she runs as if the devil is after her. At first, I was angry and then intrigued and finally I fall in love with her. We fight like cats and dogs; we have misunderstandings. She makes me so jealous that I could kill her. It is then that I realise I am in love; that the woman I can't have is the woman I want most.'

'You were equals.'

'Exactly; equals in every way you can imagine. I find that I respect her more than I have ever respected a woman. The others have passed through my mind like dreams, but she is a reality for me. So, finally, we marry and it is like living on a high all the time. I never know what she is thinking; I never know what she will do next. But she loved me; this I know.'

Marta tucked her feet under her and looked at the lines of sadness on Casmir's face. Although her experience with Blaine was different she thought she could understand some of the fire and passion that had gone into Casmir's marriage and, in a way, she envied him that intensity. She had never really had such feelings about Blaine, except perhaps when she was fifteen and dying for him to notice her existence in the midst of the mob scene at the Morrisons' house. But when he had finally asked her out they had quickly settled into a relationship that was characterised by companionship and courtesy. Blaine had never threatened her emotions; she knew he was crazy about her, and she supposed, in looking back, that she'd never threatened his in turn. He knew that she was too busy with her dancing to be interested in other men. They'd had interests in common, knew all the same people and lived next door to one another before marrying and sharing an apartment. Love had never blazed for them, but had burned with a steady, warming light.

'Perhaps you hoped that Cynthia would be another Bonnie,' she said.

Casmir gave her a smile filled with a mocking self-irony. 'Marta, reader of hearts, you are right. I no longer can treat women the way I used to; I do not have that distance anymore in myself. It is my fault if Cynthia thinks that I wish to marry her.'

Marta ran her finger slowly over the rim of her glass. 'I learned from my own . . . experience that casual sex is very unsatisfactory. It left me empty.'

'How casual was it?'

'A . . . one night stand.'

'Marta,' he said, shaking his head in astonishment. 'I find it hard to believe that you do this.'

She grimaced, 'I do, too. I guess I was desperate.'

'You need a man's arms around you.'

Marta gave him a quick glance. 'Yes, it wasn't the sex at all, but at the time, it seemed the only way to find something that would . . .' she groped for the right words, but Casmir supplied them for her.

'. . . that would fill the loneliness.'

'Yes, it's sad, isn't it?'

Casmir's voice was grim. 'It is sad for death to enter our lives and take away people we love. It is sad to be a survivor and to take solace in strange bodies and vodka.'

'Cynthia wasn't the first?'

He ran fingers through his blond hair, tousling it even more. 'No, I have a brief affair with a woman I meet at a party, but she does not understand the commitment I make to the ballet. It is then that I decide not to become involved with women who are not dancers. It is too difficult.' He shrugged. 'So I pick Cynthia for the next one, and end up with more trouble than I expected.'

'But she's gone now.'

Casmir shook his head mournfully. 'She'll be back. I have this feeling about her; it is here,' he patted his flat abdomen, 'it is a . . . what do you call it?'

'A gut instinct?'

'That's it,' he said and, in one swallow, finished his tumbler of vodka, adding when he had finished. 'It has come to me, *milaya*, that my days of being a playboy are over. I no longer have the heart for it.'

Marta put down her glass. 'I've decided that the next time I go to bed with a man, I'll have to be in love with him.'

'Yes,' he said slowly, picking up the bottle of vodka again, 'I think I feel the same. I do not find what I want with just any woman. Perhaps, I should wait for love to come, and in the meantime . . .' he gave the vodka bottle a melancholy pat, 'there are always other compensations.'

'Drinking is bad for your dancing,' Marta said in a low voice.

'A good Russian can drink a bottle of vodka and not feel a thing.'

'Casmir, you're already half-way to being plastered.'

He poured himself another glass. 'This English is beyond me. What sort of a word is "plastered?" This is what you do to walls, isn't it?'

Marta looked at his glass with alarm. 'Gregory will be furious.'

'Gregory, one must hope, is a man with a heart of sympathy.'

Marta tried another tack. 'What about me?' she asked. 'I need a partner who can dance.'

'I promise you, *milaya*, that I shall be completely when necessary,' and he lifted the glass to his mouth.

'Casmir,' Marta said quickly, thinking that as long as he was talking he wouldn't be drinking. 'What are you going to do about Cynthia?'

He put the glass down for a second. 'What about her?'

'We're on tour, and she's going to make life impossible for the company.'

'True,' he said morosely. 'Too true. I will receive looks of daggers and reproachful expressions. I already wish that I had never laid eyes on her. Tomorrow I will wish myself back in Russia.'

Once again, he lifted the glass to his mouth and this time, Marta stood up, walked over to the bed and took it out of his hand. He watched in astonishment as she also grabbed the bottle off the bedside table, walked into the bathroom and poured the contents of both down the sink.

'Marta!—what are you doing?'

'I have an idea,' she said, returning to the bedroom. It had come to her in a flash; she hoped that it would not only appeal to Casmir, but also distract him from drinking. 'You're going to love it.'

'Do you know what good Russian vodka costs?' he asked in outrage.

She sat down on the edge of the bed and looked at him. 'We're friends, aren't we?'

'I am reconsidering,' he said gloomily. 'Friends do not pour my vodka down a sink.'

'Casmir,' she put a hand on his shoulder and tried to ignore how sleek and warm his skin felt beneath her fingertips, 'this is a brainstorm.'

His blue eyes were narrowed and suspicious. 'It had better be.'

'You're worried about Cynthia bothering you, right?'

'So?'

'Use me for protection,' she said triumphantly.

'What?'

'We will make believe that we're having an affair, and Cynthia won't dare to come near you.' He was looking at her, his expression bewildered. 'You see, she saw me out in the hall when she left, and if I spent the rest of the night with you, gossip will get out and she'll figure that you took me on the rebound.'

'This is ridiculous,' he said.

Marta, on the other hand, had thought it sounded better with each word. 'No, it will work and Cynthia won't be on your back. Casmir, I can't have you miserable; it will affect our dancing. You know that.'

'And what about your reputation?'

She hadn't thought about that. 'It . . . doesn't mean much to me. I really don't care what other people think.'

He laid back on the pillow and stared up at the

ceiling. 'This is like some comedy routine. I don't like it.'

Marta wondered how many other bottles of vodka Casmir carried with him on a tour and she wasn't so easily put off. The rumours about Casmir's drinking after Bonnie's death were appalling, and she knew what alcohol could do to dancers. It harmed their bodies and ruined their co-ordination. She didn't want Casmir to diminish his own capabilities; he was one of the world's great dancers and, with an admitted selfishness, she needed the confidence he gave her to dance her heart out. She always knew he'd be in the right place at the right time, ready to catch her when she leaped, his hands sure and strong as they held her. If she spent the nights with him during the tour she could make sure that he didn't drink. It was in her own interest, she argued to herself, to keep him healthy and sober.

'Look,' she said soothingly, 'we've both admitted that we're lonely and need companionship, and we won't have to keep the charade going once we get back to New York. It will only be for the tour, and it will make Cynthia easier to handle.'

'She doesn't like you.'

Marta shrugged. 'I know that—it's natural, considering how badly she wants to be your partner.'

Casmir ran a weary hand over his eyes. 'She thought I would choose her, but I do not let my personal life mix with my dancing. She didn't like that.'

'I can manage Cynthia,' Marta said.

Casmir shook his head, blinked as if in disbelief and then grinned. 'You are crazy woman.'

'Nope, I'm perfectly sane and very selfish. I have to keep you going; I don't want to dance with anyone else.'

Casmir pulled himself upright, stared at her for a second and then, with a laugh, picked up the long swathe of her hair and rolled it around his broad hand as if it were a rope. 'You will sleep with me? Here in this bed?'

'Yes.'

'And you trust that I don't touch you?' He tugged on her hair.

Marta gave him a smile. 'Don't think you can do it?'

'I have never slept with a woman that I do not have sex with.'

'There's a first time for everything.'

The blue eyes were amused. 'Perhaps, mysterious Marta, you do want to make love to me.'

Marta looked him directly in the eye. 'I told you; no casual sex. I thought you agreed with that.'

'Oh, Marta, you are so easy to tease. You should see how red your cheeks are; fire-engine red.'

Marta could feel the heat in her face, but she refused to spar with him. 'You are a very attractive man,' she said, 'but I don't want to sleep with you.'

'And you are very attractive woman.' He pulled back on her hair so that she was compelled to turn her face more directly towards him, its oval pale and her eyes huge in the shadows. He was not smiling any longer; his mouth was straight and serious as he appraised her. Marta tried to keep her face impassive so that he could not see the effect he was having on her or guess that her heart was beating furiously, its drumming heavy in her ears. They were sitting so close together, just the two of them on the bed, the lamp casting a pool of light on to his bent arm and making the hairs that curved over its muscles glint like filaments of gold. 'I will try this experiment,' he added. 'It will keep Cynthia out of my way and, yes, because I too have loneliness and need someone in the small hours of the morning when it weighs upon me. And we will see, *lapushka*, just what friendship means.'

Going to bed with Casmir, Marta decided later, was painless, somewhat awkward and not without its moments of humour. With great solemnity and formality, she and Casmir carefully arbitrated which sides of the bed they would sleep on. Fortunately, it was relatively easy; in the ensuing discussion it developed that he preferred the right and she the left. He asked her with great politeness if she would prefer if he slept on top of the covers, but she said that it was perfectly all right if he slept under the sheets. Clearing her throat, she explained that they were bound to touch one another, but that it really wouldn't matter, would it?

Casmir assured her in gentlemanly tones that, of course, it wouldn't and, in fact, might be very cosy indeed. He recalled that one of the best parts of being married was having someone in bed with him every night even when sex wasn't involved. Marta said that she too remembered how much she had enjoyed Blaine's presence next to her; they had talked a lot, she said. That was, it seemed, precisely what Bonnie and Casmir did, spent hours talking at night and never went to sleep angry at one another, although—and here Casmir swore softly in Russian—they were capable of truly ferocious battles.

A slightly more uncomfortable moment occurred after they had pulled down the covers and Marta had taken off her bathrobe. Casmir informed her that he was accustomed to sleeping in the nude but—and there was a suspicious sparkle in his eyes when he saw the expression on her face—he'd make an exception in her case. Marta willed her pulse to slow down and told him, with as straight a face as possible, that it was truly gallant of him to make this sacrifice for her.

They climbed into bed, eyes averted from one another, and Casmir turned off the light. For a while they both lay motionless in the bed while Marta stared up into the darkness and wondered if she dared turn over. Was she comfortable? Casmir enquired. Oh, very, she answered and there was more silence while Marta began to realise that, if she could not move and could not breathe, there wasn't a chance in the world that she would sleep this night or any other of the tour.

'This is idiotic,' Casmir said, breaking the silence.

'What is?'

'You and me.'

She cleared her throat. 'Well, we're not used to sleeping together. It might take awhile.'

'The hell with that,' he rumbled and there was a sudden rustling movement.

Marta felt herself being turned over on her side and curved against the front of Casmir's body. His arm went around her waist; his hand was tucked under the bottom edge of her rib cage. She could feel the length of him; his chest against her back, the front of his legs warming the back of hers, his toes touching the bottom of her feet.

'That's better,' he said. 'Yes?'

Marta cleared her throat. 'Yes.'

He gave a small growl of satisfaction. 'Now, I sleep.'

'Me, too.'

And Marta did fall asleep, but not before admitting to herself some home truths that she would not have confided in a soul. She knew very well that her suggestion to play the part of Casmir's lover had less to do with his drinking than with her own desire to be around him. She liked sleeping with him. His body was solid and warm, and his arm around her waist made her feel comforted and protected. She liked talking to him and knowing what he was thinking; when she was with him, life seemed nicer, softer, easier to adjust to. The hard and painful edge of her loneliness disappeared in Casmir's presence, and she forgot about Blaine, her guilt and her sorrows. Instead, she had the pleasurable sensation that comes from being with a man whose physical attractions were great and whose closeness made the air seem to shimmer with a suppressed excitement.

Marta had lied when she said she didn't want to sleep with Casmir of course she did, the very thought of it made her mouth go dry and a trembling begin deep within her, but she also didn't want to be used and then discarded by a man who was not ready to make a commitment to a woman. Marta understood the way in which Casmir had dealt with Cynthia. His careless philandering of the past had yielded to love for one woman, and he had grown in the experience. The agonies of being in love had taught him to be sympathetic and sensitive, and these were qualities he had brought to his affair with Cynthia. She, in turn, confusing kindness with affection and desire with true passion, had thought he was in love with her.

Marta knew she would be spared this sort of misunderstanding. She wasn't looking for love, she thought; she needed friends, male as well as female, to fill in the gaps in her life. Casmir had a loving heart with the capability of infinite expansion, and she needed the warmth and tenderness that he brought to those that he cared about. Sleeping with him, in the sexual sense of the words, might add another dimension to their relationship, but it also could destroy the fragile connections they were building towards one another. They formed a bridge that Marta knew she desperately required; a bridge to sanity, to wholeness and to happiness. Nothing in this world, she thought grimly as she fell asleep, not even her own physical desires, were going to come between her and that goal.

CHAPTER FIVE

THE reckless decision she had made to play the part of Casmir's lover, Marta found, was one of the nicest choices she had ever made. Her loneliness had preyed most heavily on her at night, and uneasy dreams of Blaine and the accident often woke her in the small hours of the morning when the world seemed most grey and bleak. But having someone next to her in bed who was willing to talk and enjoyed the physical comforts of cuddling was like having a shield between her and the night-time demons. She and Casmir were quite careful to avoid any touching or conversation that had even the slightest sexual connotation, but they often had discussions that lasted for hours and would fall asleep curled up together. Marta often thought, during this time, how odd the rest of the world would have found it, if they knew how surprisingly contented she and Casmir were with their long discussions and innocent embraces. Most people would have found the situation unbelievable or highly amusing, but then they had agreed that no one should ever know how platonic their relationship really was. As far as Casmir and Marta were concerned the rest of the world could think what it pleased.

They talked about the past, and Marta learned a lot about Casmir's life. His father had been a factory foreman who had vociferously objected to his son's desire for a career in ballet. Family quarrels had led to an estrangement that was later healed when Casmir's obvious talents led him so quickly to a starring role in the Kirov Ballet. Marta sensed the strong feelings that Casmir had about his father when he talked about his decision to defect and its repercussion. It had been hard to separate himself from the culture he had grown up in and harder still to face the punishment imposed by the Soviets. He had, of course, never heard from his family again, and any contact he had attempted to make with them had been futile. The Iron Curtain had been firmly set in place.

Women, Casmir confessed, had been his solace and diversion, although he had not recognised this at the time. He had been vaulted into celebrity status immediately, and all the glories and benefits of stardom had fallen into his lap like manna from heaven. The choices had been so glittering that he'd gone just a little bit crazy at the beginning. He admitted all of this shamefully to Marta one night as she lay beside him and savoured the weight of his arm over her shoulders.

'A woman for every day of the week,' he said.

'A different one every night?' Marta asked in disbelief.

'It is shameful, this way I use them. I know this.'

'Did you even know their names?'

'Sometimes,' he said sadly. 'Only sometimes.'

Casmir had, of course, eventually calmed down and restricted himself to one affair at a time, but his attitude had not really changed. Women were for fun, for recreation and for mutual pleasure. What went on between their ears hadn't interested him at all.

Bonnie had changed all that, and Marta was thankful for the influence that the other woman had had on Casmir, thinking that while she might have wanted him in physical terms before his marriage, she wouldn't have wanted to know him in intellectual or emotional terms. The drive he'd had towards women had been tempered and refined until he'd come to realise that sex without love or caring was shallow and inadequate. Marta had learned that in one night, but then she thought that women were different. They recognised, far earlier than men, the importance of love.

They talked about their childhoods, their ambitions, their adolescence and their marriages. They talked about their futures and what they would do when they could no longer dance. For Casmir this subject was purely speculative since he was at the height of his career and had years of dancing to go, but for Marta the conversation hit much closer to home. She had had two separate incidences in Providence of that stabbing pain in her knee, and although each had come and gone within seconds, the aftermath had left her breathless and almost incapable of functioning. She had recovered quickly both times, and fortunately no one had noticed her small moments of failure since she had been dancing with a group or heading off-stage when the pain occurred, but she had nightmarish visions of collapsing in the middle of the ballet or having the pain go on and on without cease while she writhed in agony on the stage floor.

She did not discuss this with Casmir although there were moments when she came close to confiding in him. It would have been so easy to share the burden of her secret and to sink gratefully into the depths of his concern, but she was afraid that he'd want her to stop dancing or that he'd go and tell Gregory who would order her to quit. Marta had a sense that her dancing time was limited, but she didn't want to end it before she was ready, and as long as she could still dance she desperately wanted to continue.

As she had suspected, their nights together did not go unnoticed by the rest of the troupe. In fact, the news seemed to spread with the speed of a brush fire, and there was even a notice in the gossip column of the Boston newspaper about their status as a couple when they danced there. Someone had blabbed to the press but no one, of course, admitted to it. The ruse worked as far as Cynthia was concerned; she hadn't come near Casmir again, and the rest of the company speculated and gossiped. When they compared notes, Casmir and Marta discovered that they were subjected to similar sorts of treatment by members of the troupe. Laughing together, they classified the reactions into three categories; the covert glances, the conversations that died a quick death at their approach, and the meaningful discussions with friends or acquaintances who were genuinely concerned at their reckless and incongruous behaviour.

The first person to tackle Marta was Sandra who came to her hotel room after the very first night she had spent with Casmir. She watched while Marta packed for their flight from Providence to Boston and subjected her to a mild inquisition.

'Famous last words?' she asked, sitting on the bed as Marta packed her suitcase.

'Famous last words about what?'

'About Casmir. Let me see if I can remember them exactly. You didn't plan to get involved with Casmir? You had more will power? You were impervious to his attractions? Have I hit on the right combination of words yet?'

Marta calmly folded a leotard. 'I've changed my mind.'

Sandra shook her head in admiration. 'God, you're a cool customer. You've got Cynthia walking around looking like murder and the whole company is set on its ear. Couldn't you two have at least waited until we got back to New York? Being on tour is like being in a fishbowl.'

Marta aimed for a light-hearted response. 'How about . . . the urge was upon us and we couldn't resist?'

But Sandra refused to bite. 'I'd like to believe you, but you don't strike me as that sort of person.'

'What about Casmir?'

'Oh, he's the impetuous type, but not you, Marta. You tend to look before you leap.'

Marta put the leotard in her suitcase. 'I realised that I'm very attracted to Casmir.'

Sandra leant back against the headboard of the bed and put the tips of her fingers together so her hands formed the shape of a pitched tent. 'You know,' she said as she stared at her fingernails, 'there's something about this whole thing that strikes me as very peculiar, but I can't quite figure it out.'

Marta took a deep breath and said, 'It isn't unusual for partners to sleep together; sometimes it enhances their dancing.'

Sandra frowned. 'Is that why you're doing it?'

Marta saw that she couldn't fob Sandra off with flippant answers. Since the discussion they had had in the plane, they had grown much closer to one another. Marta had even talked to Sandra a bit about Blaine, no longer afraid that the other woman would blab to the whole company. She had learned that Sandra gossiped about people she didn't care about or did not like, but as a friend she was loyal and close-mouthed. Marta knew that her astonishment and confusion came out of the friendship they shared; Sandra could not for the life of her understand why Marta had plunged into a relationship with Casmir. Never in all their conversations had Marta even so much as hinted at any sexual interest in him.

She couldn't tell Sandra the absolute truth, but she could offer her a partial explanation that did have an element of truth to it. 'I'm lonely, I guess. I've been widowed for two years.'

Sandra was all sympathy. 'Marta, I can understand that, but you know what Casmir is like. His reputation isn't the most savoury and look at how he dropped Cynthia like a hot potato. He didn't even wait a decent amount of time before taking you on. There isn't any hope of this relationship going anywhere, and if you're looking for a long-term commitment you're going to be hurt and disappointed.'

Marta picked up another leotard. 'I went into this with my eyes open.'

Sandra sighed and tried another tack. 'I know what it's like to be the one who's left behind, but I don't think you do. You had a good marriage with a sweet guy who adored you. You're very trusting, Marta, and it makes you vulnerable to a charming heel like Casmir.'

'I'm not planning on falling in love with him.'

'People don't plan to fall in love; their hearts get

caught when they're not looking.' Sandra put out her hands in a pleading gesture. 'It happened to me, Marta. I didn't *plan* on loving Guy. I thought I'd have some fun and some companionship; I didn't intend to get involved, but I did. And look where it left me; high and dry and unhappy. He made me more miserable than I'd ever been in my life. I'd never thought a man could have so much power over me.'

'Oh, I wouldn't let Casmir have that sort of power.'

'It will develop that way, you'll see. You'll want to please him and keep him near you, and the next thing you know, jealousy will be part of your everyday life.'

Marta gave her a nonchalant shrug. 'Maybe there will be a reversal; maybe Casmir will become jealous of me.'

Sandra gave a short, unamused laugh. 'That'll be the day. Frankly, I think he's a one-woman man, and when Bonnie died, that was that.'

Marta straightened up and stared at Sandra for a moment before turning away. A one-woman man. She'd never thought about Casmir in those terms, but Sandra might be right. There were men like that who were capable of focusing their love and allegiance on only a single woman. 'I guess,' she said, 'that I'll have to take my chances.'

'But. . . .'

Marta turned back, determined to find a way out of this conversation. She didn't like deceiving Sandra, and it made her uncomfortable to lie with such frequency. She decided to fall back on humour. 'Really, Sandra,' she said with a teasing smile. '"Doth the lady protest over much?" Do I detect the slightest bit of envy? You once told me that you wouldn't resist if Casmir made a pass at you.'

As she had expected, Sandra rose to the bait. 'Well,' she drawled, giving Marta a mock-meaningful look, 'if he lay on my bed and said "take me, take me", I don't suppose I'd *refuse*.'

'There, you see.'

'Just tell me one thing then.'

'Mmm?'

'Is it worth it?' Sandra asked archly.

Marta only wished that Casmir was present to see her roll her eyes as if in ecstasy and to hear her answer. 'You'd better believe it,' she said. 'It's worth every minute.'

Sandra accepted Marta's decision and said nothing more about it, but Gregory was in a regular stew. He cornered her in Boston's Logan airport and insisted that she have coffee with him. He hemmed and hawed for awhile, took several flying leaps into discussions of the weather and the coming schedule, and then got down to business, his hands twisting his coffee spoon and his eyes on some point just beyond her right shoulder.

'It has come to my attention,' he said, 'that you have . . . that you and Casmir are seeing one another.'

What an interesting way of putting it, Marta thought. 'Yes,' she said, suppressing a smile.

Gregory furiously stirred his coffee. 'Frankly, I prefer not to interfere in these matters. You're not children.'

'No,' she said.

'But on the other hand, I have a ballet company to think about.'

'Oh, I understand that.'

'Now, I probably wouldn't have even bothered mentioning this if it weren't for Carrie, but . . . ahem. . . .' his throat seemed quite clogged.

'Yes?'

'She did this once to me, you see, and it threw an entire schedule out of whack.'

Marta could see that throwing an entire schedule out of whack was a grave sin in Gregory's book. 'Did what?' she asked.

He did not answer directly, but clear his throat. 'A member of the corps is one thing, but a prima ballerina is another. You can see that, I'm sure.'

'See what?' Marta asked innocently.

'That it would set the company back. I mean Donleavey is a fine dancer, but she really couldn't replace you, not really.'

Marta was highly amused by the fact that, despite his obvious discomfort in talking to her, Gregory believed it was his responsibility to her, to the company and to the greater glory of ballet to make sure that she was aware of the risks she was taking, but she did not have the heart to string him out any longer.

'Gregory, you don't think I'd be foolish enough to get pregnant, do you?'

Even his bald head went red. 'It's . . . ahem, not uncommon.'

'I was a married woman,' she protested.

'Well, I know that, and I was fairly sure that you knew what you were doing but I just felt that I had to . . . remind you of eventualities and possibilities.' His throat-clearing stopped after this, and Marta could see that five-syllable words had a way of comforting him. 'Carrie might not bounce back as quickly as she thinks, and you and Casmir are doing such a fine job that I have hopes you'll dance together during the regular season.'

Marta gave him a smile. 'I'd like that,' she said.

'I thought you might,' he said gruffly.

She couldn't resist the urge to pat him on one plump hand. 'And don't worry about me,' she said soothingly. 'I can take care of myself.'

The most surprising reaction of all came from a totally unexpected corner. Marta had come down to the hotel lobby in Boston to buy a newspaper. A tour, she had come to realise, was totally time-consuming. She not only had no time to sightsee, she could rarely remember what city she was in and, as for the outside world, it might as well not have existed at all. Although the company was not in New York, they still had class in the morning and a brush-up rehearsal in the afternoon, sometimes in space donated by a local ballet school or at the theatre if it had the equipment. They rested, had dinner and had to report at the theatre two hours before a performance to warm-up and get in their costumes. Even minutes before a dancer was due on stage she might be found doing pliés and tendus in the wings. That sort of warm-up was not only necessary to maintain flexibility but also was an insurance against muscular and ligament injury from dancing with cold muscles.

As she paid for her paper Marta felt a touch on her arm and turned to find Cynthia standing beside her. The other dancer looked pale but composed, dressed as Marta was in jeans and a pullover.

'I'd like to talk to you for a minute, if you don't mind,' she said.

Marta was taken aback. 'I . . . of course. Where do you want to go?'

Cynthia indicated a loveseat in one corner of the lobby where they could talk without anyone overhearing them and they would be shielded from curious eyes by a large and decorative fern. Marta nodded her head and followed the other woman, watching the slight figure before her and trying to figure out what Cynthia was going to say. Was she going to be abusive, critical, snide or jealous? Was she going to beg for Casmir back or tell Marta she could have him on a golden platter? Marta didn't expect the conversation to be anything but unpleasant. She knew how Cynthia felt about her.

They sat down on the loveseat, each leaning against an arm rest and facing one another. Marta could see that Cynthia had not got much sleep during the past few nights. There were mauve shadows under the hazel eyes and lines of strain that ran from nose to mouth. She had an air of fragility that looked ethereal on the stage and bone-weary under the flourescent lights of the lobby. Marta knew that, in comparison, she looked well-rested and content; she was sleeping better than she had in months.

'This isn't easy for me,' Cynthia began.

'There's no need to. . . .'

The other woman spoke quickly as if she were afraid that she would lose her courage. 'No, I want to, and I want you to know that I'm not speaking because I'm angry or jealous.' Marta must have looked sceptical, because she added, 'I was, but I'm not anymore.'

'I believe you,' Marta said quickly, 'so you don't have. . . .'

Cynthia grimaced and shook her head. 'I wasn't surprised when I found out that you had . . . spent the night with Casmir after I left. He's always liked you and thought very highly of you. I never really meant much to him.'

'Cynthia. . . .'

'It's all right; I don't love him, but no woman likes to have a man turn to someone else, and . . . well, I had intended to go back to him in the morning and patch it up. I thought we were just having a lover's tiff; I didn't think we'd actually ended things.'

So Casmir had been right to think that Cynthia would want him back. Marta aimed for a diplomatic lie. 'He thought you wanted out.'

Cynthia gave an unhappy shrug. 'I did at the time, but I was angry and said things I've since regretted.'

Marta felt totally inadequate to the situation. She had been able to imagine how Cynthia felt, but she didn't want to know in facts and details. She didn't want to think that her happiness rested on someone else's misery. 'I . . . I'm sorry,' she began in a faltering tone.

'I don't want your apologies,' Cynthia said quickly. 'And I don't want to talk about myself, but I learned something in my time with Casmir that I thought you should know.' She lifted a hand so that Marta would not speak. 'Oh, I'm not going to reveal any intimate details; I'll spare you that, but I wanted to warn you about his wife.'

The mention of Casmir's dead wife was the last thing Marta expected to hear. 'Bonnie?' she asked incredulously.

'None other,' Cynthia said bitterly. 'She'll haunt you; take my word for it. He's never forgotten her and I think he still loves her. I can guarantee that she'll drive you crazy. Once Casmir even called out her name when we were in bed together.'

A one-woman man, Sandra had said. 'I know he was devoted to her,' Marta said slowly.

Cynthia shook her head with vehemence. 'This goes further than devotion, believe me. I don't think any woman will usurp her place, and she's probably far more powerful dead than alive. You can't compete with her; you'll never be more beautiful or sexier or alluring than the vision Casmir is carrying around in his memories.'

'I . . . hadn't thought of that.'

'I won't pretend that I like you,' Cynthia said, 'but I've got to the point about Casmir where I actually feel sorry for you. And I know I'm better off without him; I want a man who isn't obsessed with a ghost.' She stood up and looked down at Marta who was staring off into space, her eyes thoughtful. 'So I want to wish you good luck. I think,' she added with heavy emphasis, 'you're going to need it.'

Although she related her conversations with Sandra and Gregory to Casmir, Marta did not pass on what Cynthia had said to her or even let him know that they had talked. She pondered Cynthia's words, unable to decide whether the other woman's opinion was valid or not. Casmir might be obsessed with his memories of Bonnie, but he also may have used them, to keep Cynthia at arm's length. The dead woman might have been a shield against a commitment he wasn't ready to make, or she may have simply slipped into his mind during a moment of intimacy so achingly familiar that he hadn't been able to keep her away. Lovemaking was, after all, the same combination of bodies even if it was done with different faces. Marta could remember how Blaine had come into her mind the night she had made love to a stranger. The other man had caressed her in a way Blaine had once done, and the memory had come to her unbidden and unwanted despite her efforts to keep it at bay. No, Marta was not at all sure that Casmir was obsessed with Bonnie. She had a feeling that he had spoken Bonnie's name in bed by mistake and used her memory as a defence. Marta could understand that; she had used Blaine to keep life at a distance for months.

She hardly thought about him now, she realised; hours went by in which she forgot she'd even been married once. Company class, rehearsals and performances were different now that she and Casmir were sharing a secret. For the benefit of those they were deceiving, they now acted like inseparable lovebirds. It was a role to which Casmir brought a wealth of experience and the instincts of a ham. Marta found herself subject to flirtatious looks, remarks and handling. Casmir always made sure they were touching; his arm would wind itself around her waist as they went into the hotel dining room, he held her hand while they waited to be cued on stage, and once he kissed her in full view of the company and the stagehands at the end of a performance after the curtain had closed.

He was, Marta thought, totally incorrigible; enjoying himself to the hilt, loving the role of lover, loving the way he could flaunt his masculinity in the eyes of the world. She was far less demonstrative, but then she had a reputation for being aloof and Casmir more than made up for her reserve. She certainly had not been prepared for his behaviour. In the beginning he had shocked her, particularly with that passionate kiss at the end of *Le Corsaire* when the curtain was lowered.

She had drawn away from him, her eyes wide with surprise, and he had looked down at her, grinning as he said, 'We are lovers, remember?' She had given a slight shake of her head, thinking of all those watching in the wings, but he had ignored that, pulled her up to him so that she was standing on point and bent her slightly over his arm so that her plait swung free and she was forced to grab on to his shoulders for balance. The kiss had been long and very thorough, his tongue probing her mouth, its sweetness mixing with her own. She had forgotten about Gregory standing just off stage or the lighting men scurrying backstage or the audience clapping beyond the curtain. She had felt the sensitive tips of her nipples rise beneath the gauzy fabric of her costume to meet the pressure of his chest, and that trembling had begun, the flutter of desire that made its start in her groin and expanded until she felt its pulse beating in her ears.

He had let go of her as soon as the curtain began to rise, winking at her as if they both were enjoying a great lark and then bowing before the audience who had risen to their feet in a standing ovation. It had taken Marta a few seconds to adjust to reality and, if she had not been supported by Casmir's hand under her elbow, she was not sure she could have managed the deep curtsey she gave the sea of faces in front of her. There was applause from the wings as well but, from the grinning faces of the company who had been watching, she could see that their congratulations had nothing to do with the quality of the pas de deux, but were being bestowed for that very passionate and romantic demonstration.

Although she was thankful that there were no more such kisses, Marta could not help liking Casmir's attentive display and understood, even better than she had before, his great appeal for women. He had that knack of making the woman of his affections feel as if she were the centre of the universe around which the earth, sun and stars revolved. It was like standing in a spotlight or being bathed by the rays of a sun. Marta had never experienced anything quite like it and, without being aware of it, she blossomed under that extravagant and exuberant warmth.

Her skin glowed with health; her hair took on a gleam and lustre it had lacked, its black now rich and satiny. She had let it grow so that it now hung below her shoulders to the middle of her back like a heavy curtain. Her eyes were no longer shadowed; the dark circles beneath them were gone. She often smiled now, and those around her responded to it, smiling back, teasing her, laughing with her. The Marta of the past whose temperament had been sunny and carefree had come back, if not totally, at least in part. Her happiness showed not only in her demeanour, but also in her dancing. She now brought to her formidable technique a lyricism that she had not possessed before. Gregory commented on it, Casmir remarked on it, the critics loved it.

Her sense of well-being was fed by a dream that came to her almost every night. She dreamed that she was walking by a river, dressed in a Victorian wrapper, a long gown made of blue cashmere, its bodice prim at the neck, its front covered from waist to hem with gradually widening cream lace ruffles. To complete the picture, she always carried a matching blue parasol and would idly walk under the long sweeping branches of willow trees that dappled the river with rippling shadow-fingers.

The sun was so brilliant and the water so inviting that she would decide to undress, loosening the wrapper at her neck and slipping out of it. She was naked beneath and, where the rays of the sun touched her skin, it would turn her from ivory to gold. She would enter the river then, wading slowly into the warm water until it reached the level of her breasts. Then she would reach out her arms wide and turn to face the man who was coming towards her, his body shimmering in the sun. The water broke around him, glittering diamonds of reflected sun scattering as he came. His gold hair was burnished to a high sheen, his shoulders were broad and bronzed. When he took her in his arms, she had a sensation of happiness so intense and so high that she turned molten, melting, flowing. . . .

The dream always vanished at this point, and Marta would shift restlessly in her sleep for a few minutes. She did not actually remember the dream during her waking hours, but wisps of it remained with her; the warmth of the sun, the embrace of the river, the joyous desire she had felt in Casmir's arms. Its darker side was suppressed deep into her subconscious. Marta could not, at this time, have faced the urgent longings of her body. They surfaced in the protective curve of the night and vanished in the light of day. She had no recollection of the sharp thrust of sensuality that made her yearn at night for the man who lay so platonically beside her.

When she looked back on this very short period of her life Marta was to see it as a moment of idyllic peace and enchantment. Her legs stopped bothering her, the Boston audiences raved about her and she felt as if she could dance forever, her energies flowing from some inexhaustible source. And the days were balanced by the nights. Evenings when she and Casmir talked, played cards and slept together like two children. He had found Gregory's concern over a possible pregnancy very amusing and was apt to tease her when they pulled down the covers and turned off the lights. But one night, she asked Casmir if he and Bonnie had ever thought about having children, and he grew serious.

'She didn't want them,' he said.

'She didn't like children?'

'She liked them, but she didn't think she could be a good mother.'

'What an odd thing to believe.'

'She came from a broken home. She did not know the proper way for a mother to act.'

Marta thought about Simone's brand of mothering and could sympathise with Bonnie. If she hadn't been taken care of by Peggy Morrison, she wouldn't have known the first thing about being a mother. 'Did you want children?' she asked.

'Yes, it was the bone between us.'

'Bone? Oh, bone of contention.'

'I want children,' he said. 'I leave a family behind in Russia and I want one of my own. We have blazing arguments over this many, many times.'

'Do you think it would have ever been resolved?' she asked.

He shrugged his broad shoulders. 'I had the intention of wearing her down, like water dripping on a stone. I do not intend to grow old without children.'

Marta could understand the depth of Casmir's feelings. During their talks, she'd come to realise what family meant to him. Unlike some dancers whose lives were controlled and run by the ballet company, Casmir held a part of himself aloof from its hierarchy and rules. He was the only foreigner in the company and the only one who had been wrenched from his background. He could not go home on vacations or have his parents cheer him on during a performance. The small, closed world of ballet was far too restrictive for him.

'And you, Marta? Do you and Blaine wanted children?'

Marta plumped one of the pillows. 'I . . . we hadn't really decided, I guess. It was too far off in the future.'

Casmir did not notice her averted face or her evasion. 'You were too young then, *lapushka*, to think of such things.'

She had not told him the truth, but this was one truth that Marta had suppressed long ago. Children were a subject that she and Blaine had also discussed, although in the beginning of the marriage the topic had been handled casually and without strain. Blaine had assumed they would have children at one point and, while he did not push her about it, Marta knew what his wishes were. She, on the other hand, was ambivalent, knowing a pregnancy and birth would interrupt her career, and she was far too ambitious to relinquish any gain she had made for a baby. She had thought that someday she would have a child, she liked them after all, but that someday was far off in the hazy distance of her late thirties.

Further discussions about children had begun, quite academically, about two years after they were married. Marta was, as usual, completely wound up in the dance season while Blaine's abilities at the bank had earned him a promotion. His new job, with its higher salary and greater security, had stirred his mind to thoughts of the future, to buying a house rather than renting an apartment and to starting a family. Marta could, in abstract terms, understand that Blaine came from a large, happy family and wanted to have one of his own, but in practical terms it meant that she would have to give up dancing for at least a year when she counted the autumn to spring season and then the summer holidays.

So she had brushed off his talk of children in a casual way. They had not been married that long, after all, they were still far from financially solid, and Blaine's remarks had been more pipe-dreams than anything else. During the next two years, Marta had been aware that Blaine thought about raising a family but they had not discussed it again. She became a soloist and then principal dancer with the Syracuse company, working ever harder and for longer hours. Without complaint, Blaine took over most of the household duties; he cleaned, did the washing and made the meals. He drove her to the theatre on performance nights and waited backstage to bring her home. He was enthusiastic and supportive and loving, and the other dancers had enviously told Marta that she was married to a 'gem'. She had agreed, of course, knowing how lucky she was to have a man who was so willing to adjust to her schedule.

In the fourth year of their marriage, however, he mentioned children again, this time with greater emphasis and determination. By this time Marta was not only starring in roles with her home company, but had had tentative offers from other companies to be a guest star and the dance media was starting to take notice of her technique, her line and her grace. Glory beckoned only around the corner, and she had quickly dismissed children as 'unrealistic now' and 'out of the question'. For the first time, she had seen Blaine get upset and for several days after their initial discussion they had not spoken to one another, he had not been there to pick her up at the theatre, and he had made sure that he was gone in the morning before she woke up.

Confused by his change of behaviour and more upset than she liked to admit, Marta had worked hard at repairing the crack in her marriage. She had spent her day off cleaning the house and baking. She had met Blaine at his office at the end of the day and suggested that they go out to dinner. They had had an intimate dinner by candlelight in an expensive and luxurious restaurant and then gone home and made love with an abandon that had not usually characterised their nights together. Blaine had been enchanted with her, loving the attention she was lavishing on him and completely distracted from the subject of children.

It had not risen again for several months. Blaine had not mentioned starting a family at all until the fateful night in the car when they had argued, their voices getting louder, Blaine's face tight with fury, his concentration no longer on the icy road ahead but on trying to convince her that she was being selfish, egotistical, hateful. The truck had come upon them seemingly out of the blue, its headlights cutting across the blackness in front of them like two sharp spears. Blaine had slammed on the brakes, but he was too late. They had skidded wildly, the back end of the car fishtailing, the cab of the truck looming at them, into them, glass shattering, metal crumpling like paper, Marta hearing her own voice rising to a horrendous scream. . . .

Casmir clicked off the lights as they both got into bed, and Marta turned to him, desperately seeking forgetfulness in the warmth of his skin, the comfort of his arm circling her, his breath rustling her hair, the even tempo of his heartbeat a steady reassurance of calm and peace and serenity.

'Marta? What is this?' He was looking down at her, his face a pale oval in the darkness.

'Nothing. I. . . .'

His voice was low. 'You wish to make love with me?'

'No, that wouldn't help. It wouldn't work.'

His hand caressed her hair, his fingers running through the thick strands at her temple. 'We are friends. There is no harm.'

'No, I don't need . . . that now.'

'Ah,' he said with sudden perception, 'the past she has come to haunt you.'

'Just hold me,' she begged. 'Please.'

He did as she asked, pulling her to him, her face cupped in the crook of his shoulder, the skin feeling like satin against her cheek. She wrapped her arms around his waist, clutching on to him tightly, feeling the strength of his abdominal muscles beneath her hands, the golden hair grazing her palms. She held on to him as if she were a drowning woman and he was her only hope for safety.

'Sometimes at night,' he said, 'you cry out.'

'The things I remember,' she began as her tears began to flow, 'they're so awful. I think that if I hadn't wanted to go out that night, if we hadn't quarrelled, if it hadn't been icy, if . . .' the words were tumbling out of her in an incoherent mass, and Casmir ignored them, tightening his arms around her and crooning softly a Russian lullaby into her hair while he rocked her back and forth as if she were a small child.

And she cried as she had not cried for a long time, in great sobs, her chest heaving, the tears flowing down her cheeks and into her hair, her mouth trembling against his skin. She was thankful for his tender care and undemanding comfort; she had told no one about that night, and even now, she could not speak of it in any rational way. But Casmir did not ask questions; he did not subject her to any inquisition; he merely supplied the solace that her heart ached for so badly, and she fell asleep in his arms at last, the tears drying on her face, her hair damp against his cheek. He held her for a long time until her slow, deep breathing assured him that she was no longer awake, and then he touched his lips gently to hers, sighed and, tucking her close to his side, fell asleep beside her.

CHAPTER SIX

THE accident was very much on Marta's mind as the time came close for the company to arrive in Syracuse. She knew that she would have to get in touch with the Morrisons; even if Simone had not berated her with her negligence, Marta would have done the right and proper thing. Not returning their phone calls or opening their letters was one level of impoliteness; being in their home town and not getting in touch with them was an insult of a far greater magnitude. And besides, in her heart of hearts, Marta longed to see Peggy and Dave again. Most of her fondest memories of childhood were of their home, their children and their affectionate love. She was curious to see Blaine's brothers again and wondered what they were doing. The oldest, Mark, had got married just before her own wedding, but Steve had seemed to be a perennial bachelor, and then there were the two younger boys, Jeremy and Douglas. They had both been in junior high school when she had left Syracuse, both tall and gangling, irreverent and very adolescent. She had missed them all and, while one part of her dreaded seeing them again, another part wanted very much to fall back into the family life she had once shared so pleasantly.

The company arrived in Syracuse on a Monday morning and did not have an engagement until Tuesday evening. Casmir was to spend most of the day holed up with Gregory discussing administrative details—it was clear that he was being groomed to head the company in some form eventually—and Marta had time on her hands. After much thought she decided that she would hire a taxi to drive by her old neighbourhood and, if the Morrisons' house seemed occupied, she'd drop in. If they weren't home, then she would go back to the hotel.

She recognised her tactics for what they were; half-bravery and half-cowardice, but she preferred the idea of leaving her confrontation with the Morrisons to fate rather than by awkward invitation. The only thing that she did to give herself an advantage was to take Sandra along; she needed the moral support and sympathy of a friend.

'A nice district,' Sandra commented as they wound through a suburban section of the city near the university. Syracuse had been built among a series of rolling hills that were covered with trees. Their autumn foliage was a rich red-gold which shaded the brick houses beneath them and sent dappled shadows over the quiet neighbourhood streets. Marta could remember bicycling up these streets and walking along them with school books in her arms. She could still point out the houses of people she had known; the Drurys, the Hatchetts, the Squires, and she wondered what had happened to them all and whether their lives were happy or sad. The houses told her nothing; their bay windows reflecting back the rippled image of the taxi as it passed.

'I went to school over there,' Marta said, pointing to a one-storied brick building.

'Do your in-laws know that we're dropping in on them?'

Marta had given Sandra only the sketchiest of reasons for this trip. 'No, I wanted to surprise them. They'll know I'm in town because of the publicity, but I didn't want to have to wait for them to invite me over.' What she did not say was that she thought it might be far easier to face Peggy and Dave when they were in a state of surprise rather than anticipation. The opening conversation would be filled with exclamations and quick chatter and, because of Sandra's presence, there would be no silences or recriminations.

'Let's hope they like the unexpected,' Sandra said.

'Peggy loves company,' Marta assured her, 'and the household is run on the you-never-know-next principle. That's the way it is with five active boys.'

'I wouldn't know. I was an only child with parents who worried about every step I took.'

'And they let you take-up ballet?'

'My mother had the erroneous thought that it would be all sweetness and light with little girls running around in pink leotards and making believe that they were princesses. She didn't anticipate total dedication, bloody toes and a complete disinterest in a higher education. They're still in a state of shock, and every time they come to New York, they ask me if I wouldn't like to move back home to Michigan with them.'

Marta gave her a wistful smile. 'I could have used a bit of suffocation like that.'

Sandra gave her a curious look. 'I thought you lived with your mother.'

'We inhabit a space together. She's an absentee parent.'

'And your father?'

'He died when I was in my early teens. It would have been more traumatic had he been around while I was growing up, but he was a high-powered salesman who spent most of his time travelling. Sometimes my mother went with him; sometimes she took jaunts on her own. There was plenty of money for frivolity in my family.' Without being aware of it, a note of bitterness had crept into Marta's voice.

Sandra was sympathetic. 'The "poor little rich girl",' she murmured. 'sounds as if Blaine supplied you with adopted parents.'

'They . . . they were wonderful to me.'

'Then how come the big surprise? Why haven't you told them you're coming?'

There was no point, Marta saw, in bringing Sandra along for moral support unless she knew why she was there. Impulsively, she turned to the other woman with a pleading look on her face. 'I haven't spoken or written to them in two years.'

'Two years! Did you have a fight with them after your husband's death?'

'No, it's a little more difficult than that. It was hard for me to see them afterwards. I felt so ... so ...' her voice trailed off; she couldn't confess to Sandra the real reason why she had been unable to face Blaine's parents.

Sandra, however, immediately grasped on to a logical answer. 'They reminded you of what you'd lost. Oh, Marta, I can understand that. I couldn't go to a restaurant that Guy and I used to frequent or listen to records that we both enjoyed. I even threw away the perfume he gave me and hocked the jewellery. I couldn't stand to be reminded of him.'

Marta was thankful for Sandra's misguided but sincere sympathy. 'I'm taking you along to help me get over the bad moments,' she said. 'Do you mind?'

'Hell, no,' Sandra said, grinning and patting Marta's hand. 'What are friends for?'

When they arrived at the Morrison house, there were three cars in the driveway and two bicycles, and Marta was so nervous she'd gone pale and kept clenching and unclenching her hands. The taxi stopped, letting them out, but Marta's courage caved in suddenly, and she had decided to crawl back into the taxi and head back to the hotel when Sandra grabbed her hand.

'Stout heart,' she said encouragingly, 'and straighten your skirt. It's all wrinkled.'

So Marta waved the taxi off, rearranged her denim skirt and pale blue blouse and marched up to that very familiar door. Her hand shook as she lifted the knocker and her heart was pounding to beat the band, but the first person to answer the door was Blaine's father, Dave, whose expression went from frowning to delighted, his voice rising with enthusiasm as he called the rest of the family to see who had just blown in.

The welcome went far easier than anything she had expected; it was almost as if the two years hadn't gone by, as if her last visit had occurred just the day before and there was no need for anyone to get too excited about her return. If Peggy or Dave were curious about why she had not been in contact with them for so long or were angry with her, Marta could not sense a thing from the hugs they gave her or their warm hello's. Peggy was in her usual sculptor's bibbed overalls, looking much as she had except that her hair was a bit greyer, her figure more stocky, and more laughter lines had creased the skin around her eyes. Dave, however, seemed much older with his hair gone completely white and very thin on top. He and Blaine had shared a strong facial resemblance, and a lump rose in Marta's throat as he wrapped his arms around her and she pressed her cheek against his.

Steve, the second son, was there since he was now a postgraduate and did not have lectures on Monday, and the two youngest boys were home for lunch. They had grown by leaps and bounds; Jeremy was starting a beard and Douglas had let his hair grow down to his shoulders in what Peggy affectionately referred to as 'student rebellion'. Even the youngest boys hugged her, and Marta realised with a pang in her heart that the Morrisons had missed her just as much as she had missed them. For the first time in months she wondered if the separation had been truly necessary. No one blamed her for Blaine's death; no one had even hinted that she might have been the cause of the accident. The Morrisons were simply glad to see her and she, in turn, was far happier than she would have ever thought possible in their presence.

Sandra was introduced, they were ushered into the house and extra plates were set at the table without any fuss while Peggy dished up an appetising casserole and home-made vegetable soup.

'Right out of the garden,' Dave said proudly.

'I didn't know you liked gardening,' Marta said.

'Dad's into dirt,' Jeremy said.

'Soil, young man. We call it soil around here.'

Peggy handed Marta a bowl of steaming hot soup. 'Dave had to do something with his hands when the boys outgrew tree houses and pogo sticks.'

Douglas, the youngest and most freckled, piped up. 'Well, I wish he'd gone into rocketry or building aeroplanes. Tomatoes aren't very exciting.'

While Dave protested amicably at this complaint, Marta stole glances around the dining room. It looked as if nothing had changed in the two years she had been here. There was the same arrangement of colonial furniture that had seen better days, the same scratch on the buffet where Mark had fallen while brandishing a bow and arrow, the same neglect for tidiness that had books piled up in one corner and magazines in the other. The Morrison cat, Batman, was sunning himself on the living-room couch as he had always done. He was a big calico cat with rips in his ears from youthful battles. The boys had had great hopes for him as the neighbourhood's most ferocious animal, but Batman had confounded them all by retiring from active service early in life. He had, in his ornery feline way, decided that he preferred the lazy existence of a house cat, and no amount of persuasion had been capable of changing his mind.

'Things are much the same, aren't they?' Peggy asked when she saw Marta's glance go around the room. It was her only mention of the fact that Marta had been away for a long time.

'Everything looks the way it used to.'

'Mom isn't one to alter a thing,' Steve said. 'I have the same dust balls under my bed that I had years ago.'

'Steve. . . .' Peggy said in a warning voice, but Marta could see how much she enjoyed his teasing. Steve was the second son, the most handsome one with blond, curly hair, brown eyes and a drooping blond moustache. Even when he was still a teenager, the girls had pursued him, calling every afternoon or dropping by the house. Steve was, Peggy had always maintained, far too interested in computers to be interested in girls, and he had not a clue how his lazy smile made the female heart throb. It seemed that he was still unattached and Sandra, Marta noted with amusement, was eying him with interest. She was not quite as blatant about it as the adoring teenage girls who used to throng around him, but Marta could tell that she was intrigued.

'You're doing a further degree?' Sandra asked Steve.

Steve nodded. 'In computer science.'

'He has plans to stay forever,' Peggy said. 'We can't figure out a way of getting him out of the house.'

'Steve needs a family like Mark,' Douglas said. 'Then he'd have to find a way to feed it.'

Steve gave his youngest brother a friendly punch in the shoulder as Dave said, 'Out of the mouth of babes.'

'Just because Mark saw fit to saddle himself with a wife and a baby doesn't mean I plan to follow suit.' Steve took a big helping of casserole. 'Besides I love my mother's cooking, and I haven't met a woman who can replace her.'

'Hear, hear,' Dave said while Peggy groaned and informed Steve that flattery wasn't going to get him as far as he thought.

Douglas was the one who brought up Marta's career. 'You're the star now, aren't you?' he asked her.

'Well. . . .' Marta said.

Sandra spoke on her behalf. 'She's it as far as we're concerned. She made headlines in Boston.'

'Not quite,' Marta said. 'Please don't exaggerate.'

'And you dance, too?' Steve asked Sandra.

'I'm a lowly member of the corps.'

'She's very good,' Marta said hotly. 'Don't let her kid you. The corps member in a New York company could be a principal dancer in a regional company.'

'Are you going to get in touch with anyone at the Syracuse Dance Company, Marta?' Peggy asked. 'I know the Director would love to see you.'

'They've already ordered a batch of tickets and I've sent them an invitation to come backstage. I've also got some tickets for you,' she added, reaching down into her purse and pulling out an envelope, 'if you still like ballet, that is.'

'I'd go to see anything Marta dances in,' Dave said staunchly. 'Wouldn't you, Peg?'

'The whole family is going,' she replied. 'Right down to the youngest Morrison.'

'Oh, Mom,' Douglas said. 'I like Marta but can't I skip it?'

'It's hard to get culture into him,' Peggy said as she handed around the casserole for the second time, and Marta was reminded of mealtimes when all five boys were at home, and the table had literally groaned with food. 'But we keep trying to make a civilised human being out of him.'

'But it's such dumb stuff,' Douglas complained. 'Swans floating around and waving their arms in the air.' And he demonstrated, his attempts to mimic ballet movements awkward and amusing.

'We're not all swans,' Sandra said. 'And the company has some outstanding male dancers.'

'Who is your partner, Marta?' Dave asked.

'A Russian dancer.'

'I read about him,' Jeremy broke in. 'He defected.'

'Is he good?' Peggy asked.

'Casmir's marvellous,' Marta answered, her face lighting up. 'He's a wonderful dancer.'

'Is he your boyfriend now?' Douglas asked innocently and, for a second, the whole table went silent. For the first time, Blaine seemed to be there with them, his shadow darkening the eyes of those present with memories that were painful to contemplate. Marta saw Peggy look at Dave and then quickly down at her plate, and she felt the blood rush into her cheeks, turning them red and making her feel as if she were on fire.

It was Sandra, true to her word, who took over the bad moment and turned it around. 'Casmir,' she said, 'has more girlfriends than I can count on my fingers and toes. He's given almost everyone a whirl at one time or another. It's part of his great Russian mystique.'

'And did you?' Steve asked her, giving her a sideways glance.

'Did I what?' Sandra answered picking up a cucumber out of her salad.

'Did he give you a whirl?'

Sandra gave him a flirtatious look. 'It takes more than a whirl,' she said, 'to get me interested.'

The dinner conversation was light after that, and the family disappeared in various directions once the dishes had been brought into the kitchen. The younger boys went back to school, Dave said that he had to pull out the last of the onions, and Sandra took off with Steve for a rudimentary course in computerese. That left Marta along with Peggy in the kitchen, and she gritted her teeth in anticipation of what was coming. The older woman chatted for a while as she rinsed the dishes and put them in the dishwasher, talking about the weather and neighbours they had had in common. It was not until she had poured herself a cup of coffee and offered one to Marta that Peggy finally sat down on a stool by one of the counters and began to speak about the subject that was on both their minds.

'It's been a long time, Marta,' she said gently.

Marta, who was also perched on a stool, looked down at her entwined fingers. 'I don't know how to apologise to you. What I did was unpardonable.'

'Simone told us how you used to stay in bed all day and eat candy. It didn't sound like you at all.'

'I was depressed after ... Blaine had died. And I never thought I'd dance again. My legs were a mess.'

'You're to be congratulated for your achievements.'

Marta looked up into Peggy's steady grey eyes. 'I should have written to you then, but I couldn't. Every time I sat down to write, I could see Blaine's face in front of me.'

'He's dead, Marta; it took me a while to understand that and accept it, but I have. Dave's taken a bit longer; he still won't talk about Blaine. It hurts him too much. But I've decided to be thankful that I have four other sons, not one of which will replace the one I lost, but they're here nonetheless and I love them all.'

'But I want to apologize. . . .'

Peggy waved a hand in the air as if to brush away Marta's words. 'I'm just glad you've come back; I don't need a lot of words to explain what you've been through.'

'But. . . .' Marta would have liked to express her guilt, to get it out of her system.

'Marta, I lost one son and, for a while, I thought I had lost you as well. Just having you back in my house is what counts. Dave and I have always thought of you as a daughter, and I don't want you to think that I'm angry or resentful. I just want you to know that there's always a place here if you need somewhere to go.'

'Oh, Peggy.' Tears came unbidden into Marta's eyes, making her vision blur until the older woman's face was simply an oval with no distinguishable features. Then she felt arms around her and a gentle hand patting her back.

'There,' Peggy was saying. 'There, there.' Marta buried her face against the older woman's shoulder, her childhood memories of Peggy returning in full force. She had always had a knack for making hurts go away, for soothing sore egos, for easing an aching heart. Marta discovered that she no longer wanted to carry her secret. Peggy had been her confessional for childhood sins, and she desperately wanted her to play that role again. Speaking about her guilt, letting the words loose into the air where they could be dispelled by Peggy's calm judgment and warm sympathy, would bring her tremendous relief.

'We had a fight in the car that night,' Marta said between sobs.

Peggy pushed her back a bit so she could see her face. 'Who had a fight?'

'Blaine and I, we were arguing and . . . he took the corner too fast.'

'Are you blaming yourself for the accident?' Peggy asked in disbelief. 'Is that why we haven't seen or heard from you in so long?'

'But it was my fault.'

'It was no one's fault, Marta. The truck slid on ice and ran into you.'

'But if we hadn't been so mad at each other; if we hadn't been yelling at one another then maybe Blaine would have noticed the truck and pulled to the side.'

'Marta, everything is hypothesis and postulation. It's useless to try and reconstruct the past and assign fault.' Peggy pulled a tissue out of her apron pocket and daubed Marta's eyes as if she were a small child again. 'Blaine's gone; life has to go on and you must live it to the best of your ability.'

'But if only. . . .'

'Hush, child. I won't listen to it. Blaine adored you and you made him very happy. That's enough for me.'

'Oh, Peggy, I wish he was back,' Marta said, her voice a low wail.

'Don't we all,' Peggy said with a sigh. 'It took me months before I could give away the sports equipment and books he'd left in the attic. It was a long time before I could face the fact that he wasn't going to walk through a doorway or call me on the telephone. But slowly the gap is filling in with other things and what's left is a memory, an image in my mind, that sudden jolt of recall that brings him back for a second. Sometimes I like to think that he died quickly, in good health and with the rest of his life ahead of him. Blaine never knew sickness or pain or misery. He was so happy he was married to you, Marta.'

Some secrets, Marta saw sadly, were meant to be told; others had to remain hidden. She realised that Peggy envisioned her marriage to Blaine as idyllic and had used this image as solace for her grief. Marta would be committing one of the most unkind acts of her life if she were to tell Peggy otherwise. She had unburdened herself with one confession, but the second one would only place an intolerable load on Peggy's shoulders. She had no right to disrupt the way in which Peggy was healing from Blaine's death; she had no right to tell

Peggy that at the moment his life had ended, Blaine was furious and wretched, that he had threatened to divorce her, that he. . . .

'And I always say that where there's smoke, there's fire,' Peggy was saying in a light-hearted voice.

'What smoke?' Marta asked, blowing her nose.

'Oh, the little whiffs about your Russian partner.'

Marta blushed; she couldn't help it. 'Oh, him.'

'Oh, him,' Peggy mocked her with a smile. 'You should have seen your face light up when Douglas mentioned "oh him".'

'We're just friends, really.'

'Really?' Peggy said and winked. 'I wasn't born yesterday, you know, and I'd be the last one to insist that you stay in mourning for the rest of your life.'

'Casmir is . . . well, important to me.'

'Now, that's beginning to sound more realistic.'

'But we're not lovers,' Marta hastened to assure her, 'even though the rest of the world thinks we are.'

'And what about you?'

'What about me?'

'Do you want to be his lover?'

Marta threw her arms around Peggy. 'You always were a mind-reader, weren't you?'

'Yup,' Peggy said, 'and there's someone else's mind in this family that I've got under surveillance.'

'Who's that?'

'Steve.'

'Steve?'

'Right now, I'd bet my bottom dollar that he's giving your friend a lecture on computers while he bats his sweet baby browns at her.'

Marta pushed her off at arm's length. 'Since when is Steve susceptible to a member of the opposite sex?'

'Since lunch time.'

'You suspicious thing, you.'

Peggy wagged a finger at her. 'Just wait and see. Your friend Sandra isn't going to know what hit her.'

It was hard to believe that a New York sophisticate

like Sandra had fallen for an upstate bumpkin like Steve, but it seemed that Peggy's extrasensory perception had been dead accurate. After she and Marta had left the Morrisons with promises to see them after the performance and to come back before they left Syracuse, she spent the taxi ride praising Steve to the skies. He was, she said, handsome, charming, intelligent, sexy, clever and didn't Marta think so?

Marta who had seen more than one female fall over Steve and end up flat on her face agreed reluctantly and warned Sandra of the pitfalls, recalling girls Steve had dropped and women Steve had disappointed. She pointed out that he had an on-going love affair with his computer and that few women were willing to play second fiddle to a keyboard and a central processing unit. She mentioned that Steve had the family reputation as a heartbreaker and he hadn't once proved the family wrong. Of all the brothers, he was the most casual, elusive and carefree. He was, she said, rotten husband material. When Sandra retorted that she wasn't in the market for a husband but a lover, Marta said that he wasn't good lover material either. His idea of sexy was RAMs, ROMs and floppy disks.

But she was not able to take the stars out of Sandra's eyes, and she realised how much the other woman needed to forget Guy. That earlier love affair with its devastating finale had left Sandra with nothing to salvage within herself. In her own words, she'd fallen for Guy so hard that when he pulled the rug out from under her she'd dropped into a chasm with no bottom. Perhaps her interest in Steve, Marta decided, was a healthy one, a sign that Sandra's heart and ego were healing. And she'd never be able to complain that she hadn't been forewarned about Steve's failings. Marta spent the whole taxi ride telling her about Steve; his boyhood, his adolescence, and his college career, each stage marked by quick enthusiasms, a bright intelligence and a devotion to computers that far exceeded any interest he had in women.

'Sounds challenging,' Sandra said with a smile as they drew close to the hotel.

'It's unlikely that he'll make the first move,' Marta warned her. 'Steve is used to the girls chasing him.'

'He's already asked me out.'

Marta turned to her with a surprised glance. 'He did?'

'Well, I did suggest that I'd like to see the sights.' Sandra winked at her. 'But it didn't take much persuasion.'

Marta shook her head. 'My advice is—don't get too involved.'

'Oh, don't worry,' Sandra said, 'I've learned my lesson the hard way. My motto is "love 'em and leave 'em." It makes things much simpler.'

When they returned to the hotel, Marta found Gregory pacing the lobby as he awaited her return. The local papers, it seemed, were interested in the company in generall and Marta in particular. As a former Syracuse resident she would make good copy, and Gregory was eager to get her primed for radio interviews, television spots and a press conference. Although Marta had not much experience with the media, she found the going easier than she had expected. The local reporters were not hostile in the least, and they were all eager to show how her experience with the Syracuse Dance Company had propelled her into stardom. They were fairly tactful about Blaine and the accident, but there was the inevitable question about her private life, which she warded off with a smile and a casual remark. When asked if she were romantically attached to anyone in the company at present, her answer was no.

'What about your partner, Casmir?' someone asked.

'We all love him,' she said with a smile. 'He's irresistible.'

Casmir, of course, sailed through his interviews. He loved the attention, knew how to make the most of his broken English and kept the reporters laughing. He complimented them on their city, which he had not seen, their restaurants, which he had not visited, and on their attracitve women, whom he had not met. They lapped it up eagerly, pens flying across pads, tape recorder whizzing like mad. As far as Marta was concerned Casmir was capable of selling more tickets than the entire publicity department of the Manhatten Ballet Company.

It was not a surprise, considering how the papers covered their coming performances, that seats were sold out ahead of time, and they danced to packed houses every night. Several parties were thrown for the dancers, including one by Marta's old company. She found it was good to see familiar faces and to talk shop with people she'd danced with before. Some of her friends were gone; they'd either left ballet or moved to other companies, but the Director was still there, her face lined and older, her hair still pulled back in a tight chignon although its dark colour had gone completely white. Her real name was Phillipa Day, but every one had called her Madame in deference to her age, her regal bearing and the severity of her expression. She was a woman of strong features and an even stronger personality, and young ballet students had sworn that she had eyes in the back of her head. Madame had had the awesome reputation of spotting mistakes even if they occurred when her back was turned. She had never raised her voice or actually shown anger, but had ruled the school and the ballet company with an iron hand.

To Marta who had grown up under her strict tutelage, this meeting held a small element of shock. Madame seemed much smaller than she remembered and far more frail. In her memories, particularly her childhood ones, Madame had resembled a large and ferocious dragon who breathed fire. It was hard to match that image with the woman she had just embraced, whose head barely reached to Marta's shoulder and whose bones seemed tiny and fragile.

'So, Marta, you come back in triumph,' Madame said as they stepped apart.

Madame so rarely gave compliments that Marta did not know how to handle one even as oblique as this. 'I'm glad you enjoyed the ballet.'

'Your skills have grown immensely.'

'I give you credit,' Marta replied. 'Every day I give thanks for those years at the barre.'

Madame shook her head. 'No, I didn't teach you what you know now. You were an undisciplined dancer in those days.'

Marta blinked in surprise. 'Undisciplined?' she echoed, thinking of the long hours she had spent in training, the days of rehearsals, the constant strain to achieve technical ability.

'It wasn't until after that accident that you settled down and really learned to dance.' Madame smiled at Marta's look of astonishment. 'You think I'm crazy, don't you? But I'm not, child. You were light-hearted and carefree when you danced with us, but you didn't really take your dancing as seriously as you might have. Everything had been handed to you on a platter; life was far too easy for you.'

'But I was starting to get reviews and nibbles from other companies.'

'I'm not saying you didn't have talent. Your frame of mind wasn't quite right. You were very comfortable with your husband and your safe little niche with us. But the accident threw you out into the harsh world and you survived. You're a better dancer for it, Marta. I watched you tonight.'

Marta had never thought of her attempt to rise out of her depression and to get beyond the guilt that weighed her down as anything more than a struggle she had survived, a battle that she had won. It was true, as Madame had said, that many of the good things in life had been handed to her on a platter. Her talent in ballet had been obvious from the time she was seven. She had sailed through her classes, starred in recitals and entered the Syracuse company at sixteen, one of the youngest they had ever accepted. Her tenure in the corps had been short and she had been given a soloist's role when she was nineteen. She had been a big fish in a small pond and, when she looked beyond that pond, she had seen only greater glories to come. Now, as she thought about Madame's judgment of her, she could see that she had had the arrogance of youth coupled with the blindness of egotism. She had been good, it was true, but she had not been quite good enough.

Madame rarely gave praise, even to prize students who had made it big, and Marta cherished this final acknowledgment of her dancing, but she suspected that the Director was praising far more than her technical expertise or her lyrical style. What Madame had really said was that Marta had finally grown up, that she was no longer being babied by friends and relatives and cheered on by a local crowd that had adopted her as their 'ballerina'. Making it in Manhatten had meant hard work without applause, pain without respite and a gritty stamina that had come from Marta herself. No one had aided her on this trip upwards; there had been no helping hands, no shoulders to cry on, no friendly faces for sympathy. She had done it all herself and it showed.

'Thank you, Madame, it's kind of you to say so.'

'Your partner, the Russian, is outstanding.'

Marta nodded; Casmir's brilliance showed in every step he took.

'He could make a ballerina look good in spite of herself,' Madame went on, 'but you must not rely only on him.'

'Oh, I don't.'

Madame gave her a look out of her frosty blue eyes and tapped her on the shoulder in a gesture reminiscent of the old days when a student required a slight amount of chastisement. 'You have a chance to be very, very good, Marta. Perhaps even one of the world's great ballerinas. It's important that you keep working, do you understand?'

'Yes, Madame.' She understood only too well. Praise

was all fine and well, but Marta was not to rest on her laurels; there were always higher achievements for which to strive, greater goals of lyricism or interpretation or technique. In the domain of Madame and ballet, there was no looking back. A bad night, a faltering step, a slight loss of ability and the critics would be on her back in an instant and she would lose starring roles. Ballet was not a world in which generosity prevailed. Talent was the criteria for judgment, and beware the ballerina who, for one second, forgot it.

CHAPTER SEVEN

THE Manhattan Ballet performed *The Sleeping Beauty* on its last night in Syracuse. Although the Morrisons had already come to several performances, Marta invited them to this last one, having obtained tickets for the coveted first box seats. She had gone back to see them again, and it had been a comfortable visit with much laughter, the occasional tear and promises to write that Marta planned to keep. Peggy had laughingly told her that a liking for ballerinas seemed to run in the family, because it seemed that Steve had been taking Sandra out after every performance. She and Marta had speculated on their relationship and then given up, looking at one another with knowing smiles. Steve's attraction to women had always been obvious, but why they hung around after the first encounter or two was a mystery to both of them. Marta had only seen Sandra at company class, where the other woman had waved hello at her and then concentrated on her barre work. Marta suspected that her relationship with Steve was friendly and casual rather than serious. There had barely been enough time for it to develop into anything deeper.

As the curtain opened on the lush set of *The Sleeping Beauty*, Marta hoped that the Morrisons would enjoy the pomp and circumstance of the ballet, its romantic story and intricate, glittering costumes. She got a lot of pleasure out of being the princess around which the whole ballet flowed, and always got a kick out of the moment when the prince, played by Casmir, kissed her awake. In rehearsal and their first performances he had barely touched his mouth to hers, but lately those kisses had become playful and teasing, and it was all Marta could do not to laugh and fall off the bier on which she was lying. At that moment in the ballet she had to remain perfectly still, her feet crossed at the ankles, one hand dangling over the edge of the bier, a rose clasped in her supposedly lifeless fingers. Lately she had taken to opening one eye slightly to prepare herself for whatever outrageous act Casmir was about to inflict upon her. Once he had licked her nose; during another performance he had nipped her ear. Tonight as she watched him approach, Marta's heart sank to the bottom of her point shoes. The smile on his face portended the worst.

'This kiss, she wake you from the dead,' he said kneeling by the bier, while the Lilac Fairy waved her wand over them and grinned surreptitiously as if she knew what was about to happen.

'Casmir,' Marta said warningly, trying to glare at him furiously while keeping her eyes half-shut and the expression on her face blank. Dancers conversed more on stage than the audience knew; they had developed the ability to talk with their teeth clenched together, their faces either set in a sombre cast or carrying a pasted-on smile.

'This one will be Russian-style.'

'Don't you dare.'

It all looked quite innocent and romantic from the audience's viewpoint. She was the sleeping beauty dressed in a white tutu whose frothy tulle blossomed with gold and green flowers. Her dark hair was spread over one bare shoulder, a gleaming black fan. Casmir, as Prince Florimund, was dressed in blue with gold braid adorning the broad shoulders of his jacket, its front and cuffs. The stage lights caught the shine of gold in his hair as he took the rose from her hand and lifted it to his lips. Tchaikovsky's score swelled around them, momentous and sombre as the ballet reached its most climactic moment.

'You don't like Russian-style?'

'It sounds like salad dressing.'

Casmir choked with laughter as he placed the rose on

the floor and bent his head over hers. Marta thought she could hear the combined breath of the audience hold itself in anticipation of the kiss. She, on the other hand, had gone quite stiff in suspense, captive to whatever brand of horseplay Casmir wished to inflict upon her that night. It could range from the most innocent of caresses, to teasing nibbles, to whispered jokes, to. . . .

He touched his lips to hers, barely breathing as their softness met, his tongue darting out to play along her lips, curving from one corner to the other as if surveying their length, their texture, their taste. Her mouth parted of its own free will, allowing his tongue to slide into its warm recesses and move sensuously against hers. Marta almost forgot that she was Princess Aurora, innocent, virginal and about to wake from a hundred year's sleep. She had a strong urge to put her arms around Casmir's neck and pull him closer, her fingers entwining in his hair.

Finally, he raised his head and grinned down at her, the music roaring around their heads as cymbals clashed and drums rolled. Marta informed him, as she rose from the bier, her hand gracefully placed in his, her body leaning towards his in a loving arc, that she planned to strangle him with her bare hands that night. His grin widened. 'Is this what they call kinky?' he asked, pulling her towards him for their embrace before the lights went down.

She was just about to answer with a snappy rejoinder when she placed her left foot on the stage. As her weight came down on her pointed toe an excruciating and agonising pain ripped down the back of her leg to her knee as if it were an animal wielding sharp, curved claws. She went absolutely rigid, not daring to breathe, terrified that it would continue, fearful that if she even so much as relaxed a muscle in that leg it would give way and she would collapse to the floor.

Casmir felt her rigidity. 'Marta? What's the matter?' he asked in concern as the lights dimmed around them.

They were supposed to leave the stage at this point, their departure masked by the sudden blackness.

'Help me,' she said through gritted teeth. 'Help me get off stage and ... please, please, don't let go.'

She limped off stage with Casmir's arm supporting her around the waist as the set was being changed. The huge grey cobwebs that had adorned the pillars of Princess Aurora's chamber during her century-long sleep were lifted off; the monstrous spiders that had hovered over her rising and vanishing up into the catwalks above. The bier she had been lying on was quickly moved into the wings by stagehands dressed in black, its rollers making only the slightest whirring sound. Slowly the lights came up, revealing that the chamber of the sleeping princess had been transformed into the great hall of the palace, the pillars now forming high, vaulting arches while great staircases swept to the farther reaches of the stage. The thrones of King Florestan and his queen stood to the right, and one by one the courtiers the royal guests entered as if not a day had passed since Princess Aurora had pricked her finger on evil Carabosse's spindle.

Casmir held Marta in the wing as the dancers passed them, their eyes curious but their thoughts far too occupied with the coming scene to take much notice. Puss in Boots walked by; the Bluebeard and Goldilocks, Beauty and the Beast, Aurora's brother and sisters, the Bluebird, the Lilac Fairy and Aurora's fairy god-mothers. The costumes glittered with sequins and formed a rainbow of colours, but to Marta they were all a blur as she concentrated on the pain that still tore at her leg.

'You are injured?' Casmir asked. 'You hurt your foot?'

'No ...' she could barely breath with the pain, 'it isn't my foot.'

'Then what is wrong? Is it a tendon, a ligament?' Injuries were commonplace in ballet companies; dancing was strenuous and contrary to the way the human body actually was supposed to move. Few dancers escaped pain during their careers.

'Yes,' she said, 'maybe that's it.' The pain had started to recede now, and she could straighten up, stop leaning against Casmir's shoulder and take a deep breath.

Gregory bustled up to them, his round face wrinkled with worry. 'Marta! Are you all right?'

So transparent was Gregory's expression that Marta could imagine the visions of horror passing through his mind. Imagine having to change Princess Aurora for the dramatic finale of the ballet. Imagine having to announce to the audience in the middle of a divertissement or a pas de deux that the leading lady would no longer be tall and black-haired, but short and red-haired. Imagine the continuity of the performance shattering like a broken picture.

'Yes,' she said. 'I think I'm going to be all right.'

Gregory's dejected slump was immediately replaced by his usual bubbly exuberance. 'You guys were great! The audience is eating it up.' And he rushed off to fight the next crisis, fend off the next disaster.

But Casmir was not so easily put off. He did not allow Marta to leave the circle of his arm, and he held one of her wrists in his strong grasp. 'What is this?' he said, thick blond brows drawn together in a frown, his blue eyes suspicious.

'I'm better.'

'This pain is gone . . . just like that?'

'Yes.' Marta wiggled her left foot so he could see its health and durability.

'I do not hear of pain that comes and goes so swiftly. One minute you cannot stand and the next you will be dancing?'

Marta did not look directly at him. Instead she gazed over his arm to the stage where Princess Florine and the Bluebird were beginning their pas de deux, one of the most dazzling of the ballet. 'Perhaps,' she said, 'it's just a pinched nerve.'

Casmir shook her slightly. 'I do not want you dancing with an injury,' he said through clenched teeth.

Marta was shocked at his intensity. 'I wouldn't,' she lied. 'I know better than that.'

'I wonder,' he growled.

'Casmir, I promise. . . .'

But Marta had no chance to make false promises because the wardrobe mistress was now scurrying up to them, her face just as horrified as Gregory's had been minutes earlier. She glared as Casmir, grabbed Marta's arm and began to pull her away. 'Are you crazy?' she hissed into Marta's ear. 'You have to get changed for the finale. Hurry!'

There was no time to think, wonder or be apprehensive about the pain returning. Marta was rushed to the dressing-room and changed into the dazzling white tutu that represented her bridal outfit. It was encrusted with gold and silver decorations on the tulle and stiff bodice. Her hair was rewound tightly into its chignon, and a gold-flowered diadem pinned securely to her head. An assistant reapplied her make-up for her, putting lines of kohl around her eyes and heavy rouge on her cheeks.

Casmir, too, had been transformed; the gold-braided blue jacket replaced with a white vest that glittered with silver and gold sequins and was decorated in a sunlike pattern of rhinestones. Beneath it he wore a filmy white shirt with flowing sleeves and a jabot that cascaded at his neck. His make-up had also been reapplied and his hair combed back from his broad forehead. He looked every inch the prince and husband-to-be, but the gaze he bestowed on Marta was less than that of a loving bridegroom. It was cold and speculative, and she shivered slightly as they stood in the wings awaiting the moment when the music would announce their entry.

'You are ready?' he said in a low voice.

'Of course,' she said, smiling up at him with all the confidence she could muster and acting as if her collapse of moments before had never occurred.

A muscle moved in his jaw as he clenched and unclenched his teeth. 'I only wish. . . .' he began, but his wish was never spoken because the trumpets suddenly spoke, their golden tones announcing the bridal pair for the final pas de deux of the ballet.

Love was in every gesture of their hands and their bodies as Casmir and Marta played out the unfolding story. He lifted her, turning her before the audience to demonstrate her beauty and loveliness and she, in turn, danced into his arms as if he were the only man present, her face lifted to his, her eyes glowing. The strength had returned to her legs and Marta felt the power of the dance surge within her, raising her to that point when she was no longer herself but someone magical and different, a princess in love, the golden sun of the court, a star in the firmament. As the music increased in dramatic tension, she turned faster and faster, her point shoes moving so quickly that the audience could barely follow her steps. When the score reached its crescendo, she threw herself forward to be caught by Casmir who smoothly moved her into the final pose of the dance, her body angled to the floor, her face towards the audience, her arms outstretched, palms up. His arms also reached outwards, and she was supported only by his bent leg and the foot she had hooked behind his shoulder. They smiled at the audience, and the roar of applause covered the fact that both were breathing heavily, their chests straining against their costumes as if their lungs could not get enough air.

'See?' Marta said between gasps. 'I'm just fine.'

Above her Casmir's smile widened as the audience began to stand in an ovation, row after row of faces rising as if in a continuous wave. 'I do not believe you,' he stated through that audience-geared smile. 'I damned well don't.'

He followed her into her dressing-room after the performance and they argued, facing one another like two prize fighters and hissing so that the dancers in the room next to them would not hear their voices. Casmir was insistent that pain that severe and debilitating was too serious to be ignored. Marta, at first, tried to brush it off as a single occasion, like lightning which only strikes once in a lifetime, but Casmir was not so easily pacified. He recalled the momentary failure of her leg when they had danced *The Sleeping Beauty* in Hartford; he mentioned several lapses in her dancing throughout the tour. Marta had not known that he had watched her so closely, and her mouth went dry with fear. She knew that Gregory was training Casmir to participate in artistic control of the company, and she knew that if he refused to dance with her, Gregory would comply.

'You want to be crippled for life?' he asked her.

'Don't be ridiculous,' Marta snapped back. 'One pain that comes and goes isn't going to make me a cripple.'

'I know many dancers who cannot dance anymore because they ignore injury.'

'I'm not ignoring anything.'

He had pulled off the bow around his neck and loosened his shirt, its white darkened with his sweat and sticking in patches to the skin of his arms and shoulders. His hair curled wetly on his forehead, dampened with perspiration that also trickled down the side of his face beside his ears. Marta was just as hot and damp and uncomfortable. She could feel wetness under her arms and between her breasts; her head itched from the pins that had secured the diadem to her hair; she longed to pull off her point shoes since a painful blister had started on one toe. She did not want to stand there and fight with Casmir, protecting her right to dance and lying through her teeth about her legs. She had fought against an urge to confide in him, believing that any revelation of her secret would be detrimental to her career. Seeing the grim look on his face now convinced her that her instinctive silence had been wise, and put her even more on the defensive.

'Marta, can you not see that this is dangerous?' He was trying a reasonable tone.

'No, I can't.'

'You are being a stubborn fool,' he said.

'I know my body,' she said.

'At least go to a doctor.'

'All right, I'll go to a doctor,' she said. She would promise him the earth and sky as long as he got out of her dressing-room and left her alone.

'When?'

Marta finally cracked. 'Damnit,' she swore. 'You're worse than my mother.'

'Your mother knows?' he asked quickly.

Marta turned her back on him and, walking over to her dressing table, sat down before it and stared at her face, its lines weary beneath the false façade of make-up.

'I ask you,' he said slowly, 'if your mother knows.'

Marta gave an elaborate shrug as she dipped a tissue into a bottle of cold cream. 'What I meant was that my mother was a nag.'

'A nag? A horse?'

Another time she would have laughed; another time they would have laughed together. 'She bugs me,' Marta said.

Suddenly Casmir was standing behind her, his hand gripping her bare shoulder, his fingers digging painfully into her skin. 'You say that on purpose, because you know my English is bad. Explain this to me.'

Their eyes met in the mirror, sea-blue to turquoise. Marta's looked enormous in their halo of make-up; Casmir's were narrowed to a slant, mere slits in which the blue glittered angrily. 'She annoys me,' Marta said coldly.

'That word I know,' he said slowly, his mouth set into a tight line. 'So I annoy you.'

'I don't need anyone controlling my life. I'm quite capable of taking care of myself.'

Casmir ignored this. 'I do not think friends annoy one another.'

'I didn't mean it that way,' Marta said. 'What I meant was. . . .'

'That you want me for only the things that please you. A shoulder to cry on, an arm around you in the night.'

Marta looked down at her dressing table, at a jar of powder, opened and spilled, its contents coating the table with a fine beige dust. She could feel Casmir's hand still clenching her shoulder with powerful fingers; she thought he could crush the bone if he tried. She had never felt so weary or fragile or frightened. 'Please try to understand,' she began, but got no further. A brisk tattoo on the door made both of them turn, Casmir's hand dropping to his side.

The wardrobe mistress entered, her glance moving from Casmir to Marta without curiosity. It was the opinion of the company that the wardrobe mistress only felt deeply about her costumes; human relationships did not interest her at all. 'I want that tutu,' she said. 'We're packing up to go back to New York. Do you need any help, Miss Cole?'

'Yes,' Marta said, avoiding Casmir's glance. 'That would be very nice.'

'I see you later,' he growled, walking out the door and slamming it behind him while Marta took a deep breath and then slumped before the mirror. How had such a fight started? It seemed to have blown out of nowhere like a summer storm that suddenly darkens the clear sky and obscures the sun. She had not meant to argue with Casmir; she had not meant to say such things to him.

The wardrobe mistress tut-tutted over several missing rhinestones from the diadem she was unpinning from Marta's hair, her broad face pulled together into a frown. 'Have to get this fixed,' she said. 'Can't have the sparkles missing.'

Marta nodded, her thoughts elsewhere, rehashing the words she had said and wincing inwardly as she did so. She was not the type to lose her temper so quickly or to say harsh things to a friend. Casmir had expressed concern for her well-being, but she had been so

frightened of his learning her secret that she had
attacked him, blindly, as if he were an enemy. Yet she
could have been reasonable. She could have simply
agreed to see a doctor, and he would have been
satisfied. He need never know whether she went or not.

'I'll be glad to get back, won't you?'

'Oh, I . . . I suppose so.' *Damn!* If the wardrobe
mistress had not been in the room, Marta would have
slammed her fist against the table in frustration and
despair. Now Casmir was going to be angry, suspicious
and on the watch for further evidence of failure. The
slightest misstep, a poorly executed pirouette, and he
would be alerted to the possibility that Marta was
concealing an injury from him. It was ironic, she
thought, that she should have felt that Casmir was a
friend, an ally, a confidante. In one sense, he was no
different than her mother or Dr Block who had not
wanted her to dance again. They were all willing and
eager to consign her once again to that state of empty
loneliness she had endured after the accident.

The wardrobe mistress fussed with the back of the
tutu. 'You can't imagine how hard it is to keep these
costumes cleaned and repaired while we're on tour.'

Marta blinked. 'It must be tough.'

The wardrobe mistress unzipped the back of the
tutu. 'I wish you could have seen the seams on the
Bluebird costume after the performance last. . . .'

Did Casmir have any idea, she wondered, what
power he wielded over her? With one word he could
reduce her to the status of a corps member again or
have her out of the company, her contract notwith-
standing. Oh, he couldn't get her fired outright, but
without any parts to dance, she'd quite literally be out
in the cold. The company class would still be available
to her but there wouldn't be any reason to attend
rehearsals.

'. . . and the portable sewing machine went on the
blink just at the. . . .'

On the other hand, Marta wondered with a feeling of

bleak despair, just why was she fighting so hard against the inevitable day when she'd be out of ballet no matter how hard she fought to stay in? If she did see Dr Block, she knew what he would say. He would be kind and paternal, patting her on the shoulder and not really understanding why she couldn't quit dancing and find another career. He really had no concept what it would be like when Marta was no longer with the company; he hadn't seen her sink into a depression so grey and vast that she'd been lost in it, a pathetic figure wandering in a fog. He hadn't seen the way she had eaten, abusing her body in self-pity and swelling into a gross replica of her true self.

'There, now, just step out of this and we'll be all set.'

Obediently, Marta stood up and let the wardrobe mistress pull the tutu off her shoulders, revealing the fine bones of her chest, the wings of her shoulder blades, the small rounded breasts that swung slightly as she bent forward. She had no particular modesty around such people as the other ballerinas, the wardrobe mistress and the seamstress. She was used to being dressed and undressed, accustomed to a world in which bodies were paramount and backstage changes had to be made at breakneck speed without respect for propriety.

'Well, it's the *Nutcracker* next,' the wardrobe mistress was saying as Marta reached for her robe. 'Dressing mice and snowmen will be a change.'

'I guess it will.' How could she handle such loneliness again? she thought as she recalled the days she had spent in Simone's apartment, staring at the walls, wandering down the hallways, empty and lost. Oh, she knew that part of her feelings at that time were related to Blaine's death and the guilt she felt over the accident, but the loss of dancing had been the severest deprivation she'd ever suffered and it had been dancing that ultimately healed her. She simply couldn't imagine a life without. . . .

'I don't suppose you'll fit in that Sugar Plum costume either. It's going to be too short.'

If Casmir gave her a chance to wear it. If he didn't take away from her the only things she really understood and loved. 'Yes,' Marta said, tying the cord of her robe tighter and pressing her elbows to her sides as if she was afraid that a part of her was going to crack and break away.

For the first time, the other woman noticed Marta's silence and her chatter ceased. 'Well,' she said a bit uncomfortably, folding the tutu with its bulky skirt over her arm, 'see you tomorrow.'

'See you tomorrow,' Marta echoed, not moving as the wardrobe mistress shut the door behind her, but standing before the mirror and watching the woman reflected there. She looked frail and helpless, her slender figure wrapped in a loose robe while her hair tumbled around her face and down her back in dark disarray. She looked, Marta thought, like a creature that was being hunted, her skin pale, her eyes wide and shadowed. She smiled slightly at the dramatic metaphor, but her smile never reached her eyes and it died away almost instantaneously. It was not so ridiculous, not really. After all, the hunter was waiting for her in the room they shared, his anger unabated, his attack being readied for her return.

She met Sandra in the lobby of the hotel or, to put it more precisely, she first passed Sandra and Steve kissing passionately on the street before the hotel, stopped for a second when she realised who they were and then quickly walked through the hotel's revolving door, hoping they hadn't noticed her tactless curiosity, but Sandra caught up with her by the elevators. 'Things are progressing,' Sandra said somewhat breathlessly. She was wearing a pair of jeans, a white turtleneck and a blue jacket. Her brown hair was flying loose, its length barely caught back by two combs at her temples. She did not look at all like her ordinary self with her heavy chignon and evenly dark complexion. Her face was flushed and Marta suspected that its high colour did not just come from the tinge of autumn that was in the air.

'I can see that,' she said dryly.

'I'm crazy about him.'

'Don't say I didn't warn you. It's a disease as far as Steve is concerned. All the girls feel that way about him.'

'I think he's crazy about me, too.'

Marta pressed the button for the elevator. 'He lives here, you live in New York. Remember?'

'I know,' Sandra said dreamily. 'It's given our affair so much more intensity.'

Marta glanced at her sharply. 'Affair?'

Sandra didn't even have the grace to look embarrassed. 'You didn't think it was platonic, did you?'

'But Sandra, it's only been two weeks and. . . .'

'Have you ever heard of love at first sight?'

'Oh, no,' Marta said, shaking her head. 'I don't believe it.'

The elevator doors opened and, as they both stepped inside, Sandra said, 'Maybe it's infatuation, maybe it's the real thing. Who knows?'

'Long-distance romances don't work very well.'

'Mmm,' Sandra mused as she stared up at the floor indicator. 'I have a theory about Steve. I think most women are simply too available for him. I have the advantage of a long-distance geographic location. What I want to find out is if he misses me or not after we go. That will be the acid test.'

'He'll console himself with his computer.'

Sandra shook her head and smiled smugly. 'I've got a few built-in attractions that his computer can't match.'

Marta thought of all the other women who had thrown themselves at Steve without success and wondered if Sandra's hopes weren't going to be similarly shattered. 'I don't want you to get hurt. Think of my guilt complex; I introduced you to Steve. If I hadn't taken you with me to the Morrisons, this would never have. . . .'

The other woman gave her an impulsive hug. 'Look,

you've warned me and I'm playing it very carefully. He's a great guy, he's terrific in bed ... Marta, you're blushing! ... and we get along together very well. I know that two weeks isn't long enough for a commitment, but we're going to write and phone and he's planning a weekend trip to New York soon.'

The elevator stopped at Marta's floor. 'I wish you luck but. . . .'

'He's hooked on ballerinas, you know.' Sandra gave her a wave and a wink as the doors closed. 'It must run in the family.'

Marta stepped out slowly from the elevator when it reached her floor, her thoughts on Sandra and Steve and the incredible rapidity with which they had fallen into an intimate relationship. *Love at first sight.* Carrie had told her that she had fallen in love with her husband at their first meeting; Sandra had obviously developed a strong feeling for Steve at that first lunch at the Morrisons' house. Marta tried to imagine what such a love must feel like but failed because she had never been similarly smitten. Oh, she had enough imagination to envision the excitement and the energy of it, but she had never known what it was like to be struck by an attraction so deep on first sight that she would have recklessly thrown caution to the winds. She had always been so careful and so reserved. She had always held part of herself back as if she were protecting a precious jewel from being damaged or stolen.

She had certainly held Blaine at arm's length and had kept him from really understanding who she was. She had covered up the deficiency in her feeling for him by being light-hearted and full of spirits. She had let him believe that affection was love and, in doing so, had also managed to deceive herself. She had been a fraud but it wasn't until now that she'd come to realise it. Her guilt over his death and her misery at not dancing after the accident had masked the truth of her feelings towards Blaine. She had felt strongly about him, but she doubted that her emotions arose out of deep and sexual love. When she'd visited the Morrisons with Sandra and then later by herself, Marta had suddenly understood what her marriage to Blaine actually represented. She hadn't merely married a man, she'd married a family, and it was that connection that had really counted to her.

It was hard, Marta thought as she walked down the corridor to her hotel room, to unravel the twists and turns of the past. She had made assumptions and decisions at twenty that no longer seemed valid at twenty-six. She had been convinced that she was marrying for love when, in reality, marriage had been her way of gaining parents and brothers. She had turned away from her own mother in the belief that Simone held no particular affection of love for her without actually knowing if this was the case. Perhaps, like other views that she's held, it was completely erroneous.

Still, there was doubt that her family had been alienated from one another. Her father had always seemed so distant that his death had made little impression on her and, certainly, her relationship to her mother was peculiar by most standards. Other families had a cohesiveness, a sort of glue holding them together at the centre, that the Coles had lacked. They had lived in the same house and occupied the same space, but that physical closeness had not brought intimacy or caring. As a child Marta had accepted her family for what it was and looked elsewhere for affection, as an adolescent she had focused her need for love on Blaine; as an adult, she had simply gone her own way. She had never once asked herself why the Coles were the way they were. It had never occurred to her that there might be a reason worth discovering or that an understanding of her parents might give her a better insight into herself.

Marta knew that she didn't trust people easily. She tended to keep her feelings hidden within and shielded from the outside by a barrier she had erected. Only when she danced was this barrier stripped away; only when she was on a stage with a thousand eyes on her did she let loose the demons of her own personal hell. This ability to express anger, despair and anguish had made her interpretations of certain roles memorable, and it was this emotional lyricism that Madame had noticed, commented upon and praised.

Most people would never bare their souls on a stage before hundreds of strangers, she thought, they would confide in a friend or a parent or a lover. But she was different and she wondered why that was so. It was not a typical trait of dancers. Sandra had the impetuosity of spirit to fall in love with Steve at first sight; Carrie Moore was warm, open and a partner in a loving relationship; Casmir wore his heart on his sleeve for all to see. He wasn't afraid to let those around him know what he thought, felt and wanted. He didn't avoid involvement and he was strong enough to withstand another's anger. He hadn't been put off by Marta's coldness, and she knew he was in the hotel room waiting for her, prepared to dig at her and poke at her, until he found out what he wanted to know.

She dreaded opening the door as she approached it; she dreaded the thought of the battle ahead. It would be so simple to admit everything, to tell Casmir about her legs, to confess her pain and her apprehensions. But it would be the end of her career with the Manhattan Ballet; of that, she was positive. And the dance world was too small. Everyone knew everyone else, gossip snaked its way from one company to another, and no other Director would hire her. She'd be thrown back in that empty, lonely world again, and she knew she couldn't bear that.

Automatically, she stiffened as her hand touched the doorknob, and she threw her head back in an unconscious gesture of defiance, letting her hair ripple down her back, its centre parting emphasising the high planes of her cheekbones and giving her face a look of severity. She took a deep breath and, opening the door, stepped into the room. Casmir was there as she expected, but he was not lying on the bed in his pyjamas. He was dressed in a pair of jeans, an open-necked shirt and a brown leather jacket. He was standing by the window, looking down four stories to the street below. He did not move when she came in and his head did not turn.

Although she had steeled herself to dislike him, to hate him even, for what he could do to her, something caught in Marta's throat when she saw him. He was truly beautiful, even in street clothes when his long, sleek muscles were concealed from view. His hair had grown a bit long on the tour and waved over his ears and on the back of his neck. In profile, his face lost some of its broad, Slavic look and appeared almost austere. His nose was aquiline, his lips had a strong curve, the line of his jaw was harsh. His hands were jammed in his pockets, his shoulders hunched slightly, a hint of their muscularity in their width and breadth. His legs looked long and powerful in the tight denim. Women had fallen for Casmir since the moment he had arrived in the United States, and Marta saw that that his attraction didn't only lie in his exoticism or his ability to make every woman feel special or his reputation as a lover. His face had never been classically handsome, but there was an inherent masculine beauty in him, its appeal undefinable and yet present, overwhelmingly present.

'I take another hotel room,' Casmir said, still looking out the window.

'Oh.'

'I do not think that we wish to stay together.'

Marta swallowed. 'If you like.'

Then he turned, and she could see the anger in his face. 'I do not *like*, Marta, but you leave me no choice.'

'I really didn't mean to say those things. You're not . . . like my mother at all,' he didn't say anything and she continued, her voice hesitant, 'and I'll go to a doctor as you suggested.'

'It is that accident,' isn't it?'

Quickly, Marta shook her head. 'No.'

'You have pain since then.'

'No.'

'You have been hiding this pain, dancing with it until it cuts you down.'

She trembled. 'No.'

'You are a liar, I think,' he said grimly.

The anger she had pushed down and away now bubbled up to the surface. 'I said that I'd go to a doctor.'

'You had better or I see that you don't dance again.' He began to walk towards the door.

Marta stared at him speechless with fury, resentment and fear, her hands clenching and unclenching at her sides. If she had had a gun, she would have raised it to shoot him; if she had had a knife she would have aimed it at his heart. The face that had once shown her kindness and generosity was now closed to her, the blue eyes hard and implacable, the mouth set in a tight line. It had happened as she had dreaded. He had turned from a friend into the predatory hunter, the enemy with a most vicious and powerful weapon, and there was nothing that she could do to stop him. Nothing. She'd be out of ballet, divested of her life's blood by one small word on his part. And he wouldn't suffer for it. No, he'd get off scot-free, the darling of the critics and the press, the company's superstar. And who would notice that she was gone? No one. She'd be replaced so quickly that her disappearance would excite only a moment's notice. The dance magazines would carry only a two-line 'obituary', and after that turn their attention to Casmir's next partner. There was a long line-up of eager ballerinas just waiting to fill her shoes.

Her fear dissipated as her rage boiled over, and she stepped in front of him, blocking the door, her chin lifting high in defiance, as a wild and crazy thought whirled into her mind with all the force of a powerful conviction. 'It's Cynthia,' she said, 'isn't it? This whole thing has been a farce from the first.'

CHAPTER EIGHT

CASMIR halted and looked down at her. 'What are you talking about?'

'You've been trying to make her jealous.'

'You are crazy,' he said flatly.

'Do you deny that you're going back to her?'

'I do not think that far ahead. I do not know what it is I will do.'

'So,' she said triumphantly, believing that she had him now. 'Then this,' and she swept her hand towards the room, the bed, the light casting a pool of illumination over the counterpane and table, 'has all been a means to an end. A stepping stone towards Cynthia, another woman. . . .' She would have gone on indefinitely, so furious was she at the thought that Casmir had used her, teasing her, being tender with her, holding her in his arms. And none of it had mattered to him; that was clear. The moment they had a disagreement, he was ready to walk out on her, to treat her as if she didn't exist, to. . . .

'I do not see what difference this would make to you,' he said coldly. 'We are not lovers.'

She blinked and stared at him for a few minutes. She had actually forgotten this vital fact. They had grown so close to one another during the tour and had spent so many hours together, sleeping and talking intimately, that she had come to believe that they were the loving couple they had pretended to be. Casmir had swept her into the circle of his adoration, and she had somehow started to believe that the feelings he expressed towards her were real instead of assumed for the benefit of others. And when, a few seconds earlier, she had actually thought he was going back to Cynthia, she had been torn by a jealousy so intense that it had blinded her to reality. Without being aware of it, Marta had begun to believe that she and Casmir were connected and inseparable. She had, it seemed, been deceived by her own web of deceit.

'No,' she said slowly, 'we're not.'

'And this is how you want it.'

'Yes.'

'So if I go back to Cynthia, there is no reason for you to care.'

She could feel her mouth trembling. 'No.'

'Unless, perhaps, you have wanted something different all along.'

The trembling spread to her arms, her legs, to a place deep within her that seemed to grow hot and tight. 'I. . . .' her voice faltered.

He seemed to have grown in stature, towering over her, his legs spread apart in a wide stance, the muscles straining against the denim. His back was to the lamp, and Marta could not actually see his features, only the angle of jaw and the slant of a cheekbone. His deep-set eyes and mouth were in shadow. 'Is it that you want me, Marta? Is it that you are jealous?'

'You'd better go,' she whispered.

Casmir moved towards her. 'I think we have both been dishonest, *lapushka*.'

She stepped backwards until her shoulders were pressed against the door. 'No, I. . . .'

'I wish to sleep with you . . . no, I will be more frank since we have spent so many nights together, and I don't use such pretty words. I wish sex with you, Marta, and you desire it also.'

She shook her head, her mouth gone dry.

'For many nights, I have held you in my arms and wanted you, but I do not touch you because you are so fragile, so frightened. But tonight you show me a Marta I do not know. She is tough, this new Marta. She knows how to wound, and I think that perhaps this fragility has been a disguise.'

Now her hands were behind her back and pressed

forcibly against the door. He was drawing ever nearer, ever closer, and Marta felt her heart flutter in panic as if a small wild animal was trapped in her chest, frantic to escape. 'I didn't mean what I said in the dressing-room.'

'And perhaps you do not mean it when you say you don't want to sleep with me.'

'I meant it.'

'I do not believe you.'

He wrapped his hand around the back of her neck, under her hair, and slowly pulled her towards him. With the fingers of his other hand he tilted her face towards his so that she was forced to meet his descending lips with her own. This time he kissed her without gentleness or playful tenderness. His mouth pressed against hers, moving and forcing her lips apart so that his tongue could enter and penetrate the recesses of her mouth. Marta felt herself weaken, the resistance melting away as his mouth, his lips, his tongue began to weave a warm magic. She had wanted this from the very beginning, from the night he had kissed her before her apartment, during every moment she had been in his arms. She had suppressed her desires night after night until she had thought they were gone, only to discover that they existed with even greater strength, causing her to quiver under the slow ministrations of that expert mouth.

He seemed to move in slow motion, pulling her closer to him, caressing her here and there, at her temple, on a cheek, running his thumb across the curve of her closed eye. He seemed to recognise the needs of her body before she even knew they were there. He tucked an arm around her waist and lifted her slightly so that their bodies matched; her mouth closer to his, her breasts pressing against his chest, her thighs meeting his. Even through the thick fabric of his jeans she felt the hard flesh and knew how much he desired her. She had not thought that he had wanted her at all during those nights when then lay near one another, and it came to her now that Casmir had shown remarkable control, not touching her then or approaching her in any sexual way. He had demonstrated a restraint that he was now shedding as if it had held him in strictures too tight and confining.

His free hand unbuttoned the sweater she was wearing and pulled it back off one shoulder so that all that remained between his fingers and her skin was her blouse. This too he unbuttoned and pulled aside so that she was bare along one shoulder and upper arm. She was breathless with anticipation, her heart thudding heavily, her breasts swelling, the nipples rising as they awaited his touch. But, as if to tease her, he did not lay a finger on her, but pulled his head away from hers and looked down at her.

'I want to see you,' he said.

She could not speak at all but looked up at him with eyes that had gone dark and wide. Her legs trembled and, if she had not had the door behind her for support, she thought that she would have sunk to the floor.

He stepped back from her slightly, reached out and pulled the sweater off her other shoulder and then down her arms so that it fell to the floor. Then he spread the panels of blouse so that her breasts were bare to his gaze. Marta had never felt such an ache in her nipples as he slowly scrutinised her, moving to one side so that the light could cast its golden glow over her, turning her skin a shade of molten honey.

Then, without warning, he kneeled before her and unzipped the fly of her jeans. She cried out in shock and put her hands on his head as if to push him away, but she could not move him. Her jeans were eased off her hips and down to her ankles, the brief wisps of her panties following, leaving her naked and vulnerable to the hand that now stroked the curve of her buttocks. Her fingers writhed in his hair, no longer trying to push him away, but desperately resisting the desire to pull his head closer to her. She was afraid of his touch, afraid that she would die of it. The ache had spread from her nipples to her groin and she seemed to have turned to liquid.

'Beautiful Marta,' he whispered. 'I have waited for this.'

His tongue stroked her, warm and soft and knowing, and Marta moaned, her hands blindly pulling at his hair, her head thrown back slightly. The tongue moved in circles, fluttered on her, pressed itself against. her. Her legs trembled wildly and she would have fallen had it not been for Casmir supporting her with his arms. And just when she thought she could bear it no longer, he stopped and she slumped against the door, her eyes closed, her breathing ragged and irregular.

He moved away from her, and she heard the creak of leather as he stripped of his jacket and the sound of his shirt being removed. His belt buckle clicked as it was undone; the zipper of his jeans made a metallic sound. Marta felt hands at her shoulders pulling off the rest of her blouse and then the sudden warmth of a bare body against hers as Casmir lifted her off the floor and carried her to the bed, settling her against the cool fabric of the bedspread. She lay there, hardly daring to breathe, as he moved beside her, his weight causing her to shift against him.

'Marta, look at me.'

She opened her eyes and saw him stretched out beside her, propped up by one elbow. The light had also turned him the colour of warm honey as the illumination touched his face, his bare shoulders, the deep cavity of his chest. The golden hair ran across the expanse of muscle, turning slightly darker when it reached the flat plane of his abdomen and thickened below. She touched him tentatively with her fingertips, but he took her hand in his and pressed it against him so that she could feel the hard heat of his flesh.

'You have wanted me,' he said, the blue eyes flickering with small flames. 'Yes?'

'Yes.' The word was said so softly that it barely altered the silence of the room.

'When?' He idly caressed her breast and she shivered.

'Since you kissed me the night we had dinner at Carrie's.'

'Ah.'

Taking courage, she asked, 'And you?'

'You will not believe this, *milaya*,' he said as he traced a warm, erotic circle around her nipple, 'but there is something about you when you first join the company that I notice. There is such a sadness in your eyes and a shyness like that of a wild animal. I could not come near you then because I sense these things and I know about the death of your husband. You were too breakable for me. I had not got over my own grief, and I need women only for comfort. I know you could not bring me that.'

She shook her head. 'No, I needed comforting myself.'

'And this I am going to do for you, Marta.' He smiled and cupped her breast in his palm. 'I am going to comfort you beyond your . . . wildest moments?'

'Expectations,' she whispered.

'Yes, that is it,' he said, switching off the light.

And he did. He made love to her with a warmth and sensuality that Marta had never experienced in her life. Blaine had occasionally raised her passions to the point of satisfaction, but he had never touched her with such confidence or assurance. He had not known what she wanted or when, but Casmir seemed instinctively to sense her needs. His mouth was tender when it touched her; his fingers gentle and knowing. He built her desires slowly, moving down her body, caressing as he went; along a delicate shoulder blade, the curve of her breast, its hard nipple. Her stomach quivered as his hand explored its muscular concavity and its rise to each hipbone, and she literally shuddered when his fingers explored the soft skin at the sensitive juncture of her thighs.

She was ready for him long before he entered her, but he had taken his time getting there and was leisurely even about this, although she was aching for him, her body yearning for fulfilment. Her legs were already parted; they had moved involuntarily, it seemed, as her desire had spiralled, but he kneeled before her and spread them even wider, running his hands up her calves, along the soft skin at the back of her knees and up her thighs. Marta's hips arched upwards, helpless with wanting. 'Please,' she whispered.

'Yes?'

'Please . . . come in me.'

The satisfaction was immediate and wonderful. Marta wrapped her arms around him, wondering at the feel of him within her and the hard muscles of his back under her hands. He moved slowly and then with a greater depth, carrying her forward with each thrust, bringing her from one plateau to the next, until she reached the seemingly unattainable pinnacle, that glorious moment when all sensation coalesced into wild spasms that caused her to moan and writhe until she gained satiation. And she felt his own urgency then and revelled in the pleasure she brought him, loving the moment when he stiffened above her and cried out, and then enfolding him in her arms when his head fell to her shoulder, his chest heaving, his breathing heavy and broken.

Happiness, fulfilment, a delicious fatigue that was the aftermath of lovemaking combined to bring tears to Marta's eyes. Her thoughts came in brief, soft explosions of wonderment as they lay entwined. Ecstasy. Passion. Desire—words that had definition beyond anything she had ever imagined. The sexual experience of her marriage had been a pale facsimile of reality, she realised, a ghost of what was possible. The man who lay above her, his body still filling hers, had bestowed upon her a gift that she had never known to exist—the depth of passion within herself, a sensual response that surpassed anything she had felt before. Her tears spilled over, ran down the sides of her eyes in slow paths to her temples, dampening her skin and slowly soaking her hair. They were a bittersweet libation: her sad farewell to the past, her joy in the present, her hopes for the future.

Casmir lifted his head from its resting place near her cheek and touched a finger to the wet corner of her eyes.

'You are crying,' he said.

Marta could not speak, literally could not utter a word. Her heart was so full, her throat was choked with emotion, her eyes were swimming with tears. She wanted to tell him a thousand and one things; she wanted to express to him the complex and overwhelming feelings that she was experiencing, but when she tried to form a sound, it came out as a small sob.

With a sudden violent movement and a Russian curse spoken between gritted teeth, Casmir pushed himself off her, leaving her body empty and suddenly chilled. She reached for him but he was no longer on the bed. She heard the sound of jeans being pulled back on, the metallic screech of the zipper of his fly as he yanked it up, the rustle of his shirt. In the dim illumination of the room, she could see nothing more than the shape of his body, a shadow darker than its surroundings.

'I am sorry,' he said harshly. 'I have forced you to do what you said you would not.'

Marta managed his name. 'Casmir. . . .'

'You do not wish to sleep with a man you do not love. You made that perfectly clear.'

The dam finally broke loose. 'It's not your fault. I. . . .'

'You cannot hide your tears, and I know what they mean.' He was at the door before she was aware of it, while she was still pulling herself upright, wanting to explain, wanting to tell him that. . . .

A swathe of light from the corridor cut into the corner of the room as he pulled the door open. 'I am sorry,' he repeated. 'I will not make you cry again.' And with that he was gone, the door closing, the room dark once again, its silence only broken by the sound of a car's horn blaring on the street below.

Marta shivered wrapped her arms around her legs and bent her head until her forehead touched her knees. She felt as if she were burning hot and icy cold at the same time. The room was quiet but her ears buzzed with sound. The skin on her bare back was so sensitive that she seemed to feel every strand of her hair, but she felt numb and empty. All the emotions that had filled her heart seemed to have drained away, leaving a black void in their place. Her mind was filled with chaotic thoughts, fluttering leaves that moved with every capricious breeze. They had made love, and Casmir had walked out. They had touched in the most intimate manner that two people can, and Casmir had left. He had guided her to a peak of sensation beyond her . . . yes, wildest expectations, and he had departed while her body still held those warm and lovely memories.

He had gone because she had cried and because he thought her tears were for remorse and shame. He had left because he believed himself guilty for her unhappiness. Marta clenched her arms tighter around her legs and pressed her eyes to her knees so hard that bursts of light appeared behind their lids. Despair washed over her in great, crashing waves. Oh, she knew that there was nothing to stop her from getting dressed, finding the number of Casmir's room and going to see him. She could explain that she had cried for reasons far different than the ones he imagined. She could even thank him for the most wonderful sexual experience of her life. It was possible that by doing so, she could ensure that Casmir would make love to her again. In fact, such action on her part might result in an on-going relationship that would bring both of them a great deal of sensual satisfaction.

But she could never reveal the complete truth to him. She could never tell him what she had been revealed to her only that night. Sandra had said that love was an emotion that crept up, taking a person unawares, but Marta had ignored her warning, not knowing how

dangerous her indifference could be. Love was as
elemental as nature, and as emphemeral as an idea. It
had no shape, but it had taken form in her heart,
coloured her perceptions and changed the way she
thought, acted and felt. She had fallen in love with
Casmir, quite accidentally and quite unintentionally.
She had guarded herself against such an invasion and
yet, it had taken place silently and unobtrusively and so
insidiously that she had not known what had happened.
What she had thought to be friendship had merely been
the first step towards emotion far greater and far more
overwhelming.

But Casmir didn't love her in return. He was
attracted to her, he desired her, but his heart wasn't
involved. Marta thought of all the opportunities he'd
had that night to tell her that he loved her if he had
wanted to. There had been a thousand moments during
their lovemaking that he could have done so and
received her ardent reply. But he was an honest man;
Marta knew that. Casmir had always spoken what was
on his mind or in his heart without hesitation. That
blunt directness was part of his charm; she had always
known where she stood with Casmir. She was a
confidante, a friend, an accomplice in a pretence.
Nothing more, nothing less.

Both Cynthia and Sandra had said that he was a
'one-woman man', and perhaps they had been right. It
was quite possible that no other woman would ever be
Bonnie's equal in Casmir's mind and that he would
never form an attachment to anyone else because his
feelings and memories were so bound up with his dead
wife. Marta knew her marriage had been different; less
intense and far less passionate. Blaine was only a dim
image in her mind, a husband that she had treated as a
brother, a man that she had married for a complex web
of reasons, not one of which had to do with love.
Casmir, on the other hand, had been in love with
Bonnie, and he had admitted that it was the first and
only time in his life that he'd ever known that emotion.

No, the fact that she and Casmir had become lovers had been unplanned and purely accidental. If they had not argued about her dancing they would still have a platonic relationship. And she couldn't forget that he was still an enemy in one sense. He would continue to pursue a course of making sure that she was fit to dance and, while she knew his concern arose from perfectly legitimate reasons, she still resented his interference. The decision to stop dancing had to be her own to make. Until she found an alternative Marta had no intention of stopping, not even if she had to forge a medical statement attesting to her health and ability. And no one was going to get between her and ballet, especially Casmir.

Marta lifted her head from her knees and stared into the blackness of the room. She was cold, exhausted and she'd cried enough. Tomorrow, the company would return to New York and life would resume its normal pattern. Casmir would not be returning with them; he was taking a plane directly to San Francisco where he would be the guest soloist for a month at the city's ballet company. His absence would give her time to think, to recuperate and to achieve mental distance from what had occurred. She'd been stripped raw and her vulnerability was painful. She needed time to mend the wounds and build some protective walls around herself. By the time Casmir returned to New York Marta vowed that she would be calm and serene. He'd never know what their lovemaking had meant to her or what she had discovered about herself. It would be a secret that she would bury deep within herself, praying that it would wither and die from lack of sun, light and love.

Simone's apartment was, as she had expected, empty when she returned. Simone was on a pleasure cruise in the Caribbean and had left a message that she would be back in a week and that the cook and maid had been given the time off. The rooms seemed to echo when Marta walked through them, and she wondered why

the beautiful furnishings and plush carpets did not seem
to alter the cold atmosphere. They were almost too
perfect, she decided, the colours all matching, the
designs in perfect harmony. The rooms had been
decorated as a framework for Simone's elegance and,
when she was not there, they seemed hollow and bleak.
It was not the sort of place Marta wanted to live in and,
for the first time, she thought seriously about getting an
apartment which reflected her own tastes and personality. She had shied away from making that decision
earlier, only thinking of the apartment she and Blaine
had shared, but now she could envision an environment
that was uniquely her own.

She picked up a stack of mail and idly leafed through
the letters, sorting through the bills and fliers until she
came to a letter sent to her by Carrie Moore. When she
opened it she found an invitation for lunch whenever
she returned. Marta put it down on the foyer table but
picked it up again. She had intended to stay away from
ballet people before rehearsals for the *Nutcracker*
began, thinking that she needed to involve herself in
something else although she had no idea what that
'something else' would be. But Carrie's invitation was
tempting. It was Sunday and she had nothing planned
besides unpacking and buying groceries at a nearby deli
that was open day and night. The afternoon stretched
out before her as an unlimited expanse of boredom and
loneliness and, after a moment's hesitation, she walked
over to the telephone and dialled Carrie's number.

To the other woman's hello, she said, 'It's Marta.
We're back.'

'I know. Gregory has already phoned.'

'Already?'

Carrie laughed. 'He couldn't wait to give me the
gory details.'

'Which ones?'

'You mean there's more?'

Marta smiled. 'Gregory doesn't know the half of it.'

'You are going to come to lunch, aren't you?'

'Well, I thought I'd unpack and. . . .'

'I'm dying of curiosity,' Carrie said warningly, 'and you wouldn't want my demise on your conscience, would you?'

'Well. . . .'

'Make it one o'clock at my place. I'll put the wine in the cooler.'

'I'm not sure I can resist.'

'Don't,' Carrie said. 'And besides, Alex wants to meet you. I've told him so much about my replacement that he's wondering why they even want me to come back.'

Alex Taylor was everything the other ballerinas in the dance company said he was—tall, dark, very handsome and extremely charming. Within minutes of meeting him Marta felt as if they'd been acquainted for life. Being married to a ballerina gave him a edge over most men who were not dancers or ballet masters. He was able to talk to her about her work and her interests and understand precisely what she was feeling. As they talked over dinner about the tour Marta thought that Carrie was one of the luckiest women she had ever met. She had a career, a husband and children which she managed to juggle in just the right proportions, and it was obvious that Carrie and Alex were crazy about one another. They exchanged smiles that were entirely personal and could end one another's sentences. Despite the twins' determined interference in the tranquillity of lunch they radiated a happiness and contentment that made a pang of jealousy shoot through Marta like a small swift dart.

'Matthew, cake is not for playing,' Carrie said, deftly removing a slice from between small fingers that threatened to squish it into ooze.

'I hear the company outdid itself in Syracuse,' Alex was saying as he poured Marta another cup of coffee.

'It's her hometown, darling,' Carrie said. 'They got a wonderful press.'

'Sit down, Mark,' Alex threatened while bestowing a

smile on Marta. 'And Gregory tells us that you got the red-carpet treatment.'

'I used to dance there,' Marta said.

'Don't be modest,' Carrie admonished. 'Gregory said you and Casmir were a sensation. Matthew, the glass is for drinking, not for pouring.' She threw an imploring look at Alex as Matthew indulged in a scientific experiment concerning milk, a napkin and the surface of his plate and added, 'You know, I've just had a wonderful idea.'

He laughed. 'That I take the kids to the park and the zoo so that you and Marta can take apart the tour and put it together again.'

'Zoo,' Mark echoed, his dark eyes growing comically wide.

'Now, I've done it,' Alex said with mock-despair. 'I'm committed. All right, you monsters, let's hit the zoo and traumatise the animals.'

The scramble down from the table was done in two minutes flat, and the twins whose usual habit, as Carrie pointed out, was to dawdle through their dressing, were in coats, hats and boots in record time. Alex had one little boy on his shoulders as they went through the door and one slung underneath his arm. 'An hour,' he said, 'that's all you've got so you'd better talk fast.'

'You're a sweetheart and I love you,' Carrie said.

He kissed her on the nose. 'Flattery isn't sufficient,' he growled. 'I expect payment later.'

Carrie gave him a reproachful glance. 'And me six months pregnant,' she said with an Irish brogue. 'Shame on ye.'

'Never stopped you before,' he said, giving her a smart slap on the backside. 'All right, troops. Off we go.'

Carrie gave Marta a grin as she slumped against the closed door, and the sounds of Alex and the twins singing receded down the corridor. 'Remember my advice?' she asked ruefully, patting the abdomen which swelled beneath her skirt.

'Give birth to kids when they're three years old?'

'I've changed my mind on that. Twenty-one is preferable—when they're housebroken and civilised.' She sighed. 'Come on, let's take advantage of the peace and quiet. We'll bring the coffee into the living room, put our feet up on the table and yak to our heart's content.'

They talked about the tour, the travelling, the hotels and the performances. Carrie, who had done it in years past, remembered rooms, hotels, stages and auditoriums with perfect clarity. When she heard about the loss of Casmir's costume and his subsequent shedding of felt leaves during the *Le Spectre de la Rose*, she laughed and clapped her hands with delight.

'I can see it,' she said. 'It must have been a riot.'

'It had its moments,' Marta agreed.'

'Poor Casmir, he must have looked funny.'

'He thought he looked like a plucked chicken. You know what? He did.'

Carrie whooped until tears came into her eyes. 'God, I wish I'd been there.'

'It was unforgettable.'

'I heard there were some other unforgettable events.'

'Such as . . .?'

Carrie picked up her coffee, sipped at it and eyed Marta over the rim of the cup. 'Such as Cynthia leaving Casmir's hotel room and you going in.'

Marta could not help it; she blushed a bright red. 'Oh.'

'You can't hide anything from Gregory, you know. He's far too nosy.'

'It . . . wasn't what it seemed. We weren't having an affair.'

Carrie gave her a quizzical look. 'No?'

'I stayed with him because he had started to drink and my presence protected him from Cynthia.'

Carrie nodded. 'I see.'

Even Marta could see how ridiculous it sounded. 'Everyone *thought* we were sleeping together, but we weren't. We were just. . . .' her voice trailed off.

'Sleeping together, but not sleeping together.'

Marta nodded and bit her lip. 'Something like that.'

Carrie took another sip of coffee and cleared her throat. 'I believe you,' she said slowly, 'but it isn't easy.'

'No, I don't suppose it is.' Marta carefully investigated the contents of her coffee cup.

'Are you in love with him?' Carried asked softly.

Marta's head flew up. 'Me? No, I'm not.'

'Oh.'

'We're friends,' Marta said quickly. 'Close friends.'

It was hard to tell if Carrie believed this statement or not. The other woman's eyes were shrewd and sympathetic, and Marta suspected that every emotion she'd had about Casmir was written across her face in letters big enough even for the twins to read. But Carrie quite tactfully didn't pursue the subject of love, instead she concentrated on Casmir.

'He's changed a lot since Bonnie's death,' she said.

'He talked a lot about her to me.'

'We were roommates, you know.'

Marta gave her a surprised look. 'You and Bonnie?'

'Uh-uh. She was divorced and living alone and asked me to stay with her. I'd come to New York and didn't know a soul and was terribly lonely so I decided to move in. We got along very well together.'

'What was she like?' Marta thought it would be interesting to see if Carrie's picture of Bonnie differed from Casmir's.

Carrie sat back and thought for a moment. 'Very independent and very sophisticated on the surface. She knew life and she knew men, but she wasn't happy underneath at all. Casmir was a challenge for her since she attracted men like crazy and, at first, he ignored her. He took me out to make her jealous and would talk to her about his other lovers. He drove her crazy.'

'And vica versa, I understand.'

'Oh, yes. Casmir was infatuated with her. She went out with Alex to make him jealous and managed, at the same time, to make me miserable.'

Marta shook her head in astonishment. 'It sounds like a Shakespearean comedy.'

'It was. It didn't seem funny at the time, but afterwards it did.'

'It was a true love match for them then.'

Carrie shrugged. 'It's hard to say. They were passionate about one another, but they were also similar in temperament that I often wondered if it would last. They seemed to have one major battle after another. Bonnie would simmer and vow she'd made the mistake of her life while Casmir would sulk and look black. Then they'd make up and the sun would shine again. It was a bit too intense for me.'

'But he was devastated when she died.'

'It was such a shock, of course, to everyone. We were stunned by it, and I often wonder if Casmir doesn't blame himself for her death.'

Marta felt a shiver go down her spine. 'Blame himself?'

'We were visiting them that day. They'd invited us over for dinner; Casmir was doing most of the cooking, but he was missing some spices that she'd forgotten to buy. They argued over who would go to the corner store and get it, and she finally ended up going.' Carrie was silent for a minute. 'And, of course, she never came back.'

Casmir had never talked about Bonnie's death; it was the one subject they had not discussed during their nights together. Marta had assumed that it was too painful for him, but she had never guessed why. It seemed extraordinary to her that both she and Casmir had gone through such similar kinds of mourning, and she felt a kinship to him that she had never felt before. 'He must have felt terrible,' she said, imagining the agony Casmir had suffered in his guilt.

'He never mentioned it,' Carrie said, 'but he changed after that. He began to drink heavily and it took a while for Gregory to get him back on his feet. He seemed to have lost interest in women although there was someone before he took up with Cynthia. I rather suspected that affair wouldn't last. She's far too young for him.'

'She thought he'd marry her.'

'Poor Cynthia, she must have been quite ferocious for you to step in.'

Marta gave her a weak smile. 'It seemed the least I could do.'

'Carrie gave her an appraising look, 'well, promise me one thing, will you?'

'What'

'Take care of him. He's a lot more delicate than you think.'

Marta was astonished. 'Casmir? Delicate?'

Carrie nodded as she put her coffee cup down on the table. 'I worry about him,' she said. 'He's capable of being hurt quite badly, you know. Casmir is the kind of man who, when he gives his heart, he gives it thoroughly. And, believe me, beneath that muscle and charming Russian impetuosity, beats a very fragile, very delicate and very sensitive heart.'

CHAPTER NINE

MARTA had spent hours walking by the river. Although the sun was strong, spreading a bright glitter over the water, a cold wind had arisen which lifted the small grey-green waves into tumbling white caps. The breeze eddied and gusted around her, whistling in her ears, picking up dead leaves from the concrete embankment and tossing them into miniature tornadoes. It whipped the bare branches of the willow trees into a frenzy, and she could feel her dress flattening against her legs, her hair tugged out of its chignon, tendrils blowing across her forehead and mouth. Above her head, the fabric of her parasol strained against its arched ribs as if huge hands were pressing against it and trying to lift it out of her fingers and up into the sky.

Suddenly, Marta saw him standing in the water, the waves breaking over his bronzed shoulders, sending spray into the gleaming gold cap of his hair. She stopped, fear and excitement combining together to make her heart skip beating for a short second. Had he come for her? He was still, his body white and shimmering beneath the water as if he were a statue behind glass. He seemed impervious to the gusting wind, the slapping water, the bony twigs of the willow tree that reached towards his head.

'Casmir?'

He turned to her, the blue eyes level and watching. 'Come,' he said.

Marta glanced at the water, its grey-green fingers leaping up the embankment. 'It's cold,' she replied.

'Come.'

Come . . . come. . . . The command tugged at her in a way the wind could not, pulling her closer to the edge of the embankment, causing her to walk down and put a bare toe in the water. It was bitterly cold, frigid.

'I can't.'

'I want you,' he said.

The words were stronger than his earlier command. She dropped the parasol and took another step so that she stood ankle deep and the water swirled over the hem of her dress. She shivered but looked steadily at Casmir's head. His hair glittered like the sun, and its brightness beckoned to her, like the elusive brilliance of a star.

Marta waded deeper, the sodden length of her dress now hampering her progress, tangling in her legs, slowing her down. Her fingers fumbled with the buttons at her neck but she couldn't seem to undo them. 'I'm coming,' she said.

'Hurry!'

She was trying. Desperately. Walking deeper, struggling against the weight of her dress, the density of the water. Every motion was slow, agonising, painful. Everything seemed to conspire against her forward motion. The wind blew her backwards, the water was like a cold wall, her own legs had gone weak and helpless. . . . 'Casmir!' she cried. 'Help me!'

He smiled at her. 'Dance,' he said. 'Dance and I will come to you.'

But she couldn't. Her legs hurt, they wouldn't move the way she wanted. Marta began to sob. 'Please,' she cried, but the wind whipped the words out of her mouth and they didn't reach Casmir who continued to smile and beckon to her. *Please*, she cried silently, *I need you. Can't you see that? Take me into you arms . . . warm me . . . love me . . . please. . . .*

Marta woke up with a snap, her heart racing so hard that her breath came in gasps. She was tangled in the sheets and blankets, and there was a sheen of sweat on her skin that made her feel sticky and uncomfortable. She blinked, but the image of Casmir was so sharply etched in her mind that she could not make it go. He had seemed real, corporeal, not a fantasy that she had woven out of frustration and desire. Marta had no recall of the dream she had had during the nights she had slept in Casmir's arms; that was buried far too deep in her subconscious, but this one had come to the surface, its intensity driving it into the foreground of her mind and awareness. It had woken her in the small hours of the night; it had caused her to toss and turn and break out in a sweat as if she had undergone incredible exertion.

She had tried to deny the feelings to herself, only to have them catch her in the vulnerability of her sleep. She missed Casmir dreadfully; she wanted him back in her bed, talking to her, holding her, making love to her. But he was in San Francisco, dancing with another ballerina, his broad hands on her slender waist, their bodies close and touching. The other dancer was young and lithe; Marta knew that from the promotional pictures for the San Francisco Ballet and, quite possibly, she was lovely enough to capture the heart that Carrie thought so fragile. Being cursed with a vivid imagination, Marta could too easily envision Casmir making love to another woman, and the thought of it cut as if a blade were twisting within her.

Her misery was deepened and compounded by the knowledge that her dancing career was soon to come to an abrupt halt. In the dream, her legs had hurt; in reality, an ache seemed to have lodged permanently in her lower spine and the shooting pains in her upper thighs were becoming more frequent. Marta fought the evidence of any disability. She got up every morning and worked feverishly at the barre that had been installed in her bedroom. She stretched and bent, turned and swivelled, praying all the while that the pain would go away. But when it did not, she finally recognised defeat and made an appointment with Dr Block. It came as no surprise to her that he thought she should give up dancing, but his vehemence was frightening. He discussed her spine and its disks in lengthy and confusing detail, but his message was plain. She was 'ruining her body', he said, and would in time be 'confined to a wheelchair' if she kept up ballet. He was adamant about this last fact and asked her if she had ever thought of having children.

'Someday,' she said, 'I suppose I might want children.'

'Well, you're not going to be able to have them,' he said bluntly. 'You aren't going to be healthy enough to carry one.'

He was sympathetic but he made no attempt to soften the blow. Marta came out of his office almost reeling in shock, and wandered through the streets near her building while the cold air and her misery combined to make tears spring in her eyes. She had counted on her body for so long that the idea that it would fail her completely was alien to her. She couldn't conceive of life as a cripple who needed a cane or crutches or, even worse, a wheelchair. She couldn't imagine a life so circumscribed by pain and handicap that she wouldn't even be able to walk down a flight of stairs or stroll in the park. Yet, Dr Block was adamant that this would be her future if she didn't leave ballet. When she thought of walking into Gregory's office and handing in her resignation, she flinched so visibly that several passers-by glanced at her in curiosity.

Was life as a cripple, she wondered, any worse than life without dancing? If only she could picture herself doing something when she was no longer a dancer, she might have a lifeline to cling on. But Marta simply couldn't see herself working in an office or going back to school. She had no money problems; her father had established a trust fund for her before his death, so there was no incentive for her to earn a living. What Marta saw as she lowered her head against the stinging wind was not the wet pavement under her feet but endless hours of nothingness stretched out ahead of her like a barren desert with the temptations of gluttony and sloth providing the only oases.

And what about having children? She hadn't wanted a baby when she'd been married to Blaine and had given the idea of children little thought since his death. But recently, a small longing had been sown in her heart. Perhaps it came from seeing Carrie so happily surrounded by family or perhaps it arose from being in love. Marta could easily imagine being married to Casmir and having a blond, blue-eyed baby in her arms. The fact that she didn't have a chance of marrying him had not quite erased the image of the baby in her mind, and she discovered that she didn't want to grow old without children. She thought of tall sons and a daughter with pigtails; she thought of stories she could tell them and places she could bring them. She had the ability, she knew, to be a far better mother than Simone. And surely, Marta told herself, there was another man in the world besides Casmir: a man who was lovable and sexy, a man who would want to marry her and give her children.

She was so immersed in these thoughts that she didn't see Sandra standing in the doorway of her apartment building as she approached and would have walked right past her if the other woman hadn't touched her on the arm.

'Surprise!' Sandra said. 'I've been waiting for you.'

Marta gave her a wan smile. 'You should have phoned.'

Sandra was breezy. 'The doorman was sure you were coming back soon so I decided to stick it out.'

'You want to come up for some coffee?'

'God,' Sandra groaned. 'I was wondering when you'd ask. I've got something to tell you.'

Marta took Sandra's coat when they reached the apartment and hung it in the hall cupboard while the other woman wandered from room to room. She looked wonderful, Marta thought, considering that she was presumably pining for love of Steve and counting the hours until she'd see him again. Sandra was wearing a bright red dress with a thin black belt that set off her dark colouring. Make-up brightened her dark eyes and minimised the length of her nose. She'd had her hair cut and permed; it lay on her shoulders in soft waves. Marta, in contrast, felt dowdy and unattractive. She'd worn jeans and an old blouse to the doctor's and yanked her hair back into a bun. She had not put cosmetics on in two weeks and the skin on her face felt tight and dry as if it were about to crack and wrinkle.

'What a place!' Sandra said, coming out of the music room. 'It could be a museum with all those antiques and figurines.'

'That's how I feel sometimes.'

'Your mother must be loaded.'

'Well-heeled is the more ladylike term.'

Sandra shrugged and grinned. 'Who said I was a lady?'

They shared coffee in the kitchen, one of the few rooms in the apartment that was not overwhelming in size and grandeur. It was cosy and painted in a bright yellow and white with a small eating nook built against one wall. It was the only room in the apartment that Marta felt comfortable in; even her bedroom was awesome with its green velvet wallpaper and matching velvet draperies.

'So,' Sandra said, 'how's things with Casmir?'

Marta put out her hand and tilted it from one side to another. 'Comme çi, comme ça.'

'Mmm—rumour has it that you've split up.'

'Oh, hell,' Marta said with a grimace.

'Can I take that as confirmation? I wouldn't want to be an I-told-you-so but, if I'm right, please let me indulge in some warm self-justification and righteous thinking.'

'You were right,' Marta conceded, trying to keep her tone light and casual.

Sandra studied her face. 'Mind if I ask you a personal question?'

'No.'

'You're taking it a lot harder than you thought you would—right?'

Marta tried to smile. 'Next question?'

'Oh, Marta, I didn't want to see you hurt by that louse.' Sandra leaned forwards intently. 'I could see it coming down the pike. Casmir's always been like that about women except for his wife, and God knows what she had to hook him the way she did.'

'You think Casmir is insensitive?'

'Insensitive, callous, cruel, a heartbraker. Well, at least you were forewarned, at least you knew what might happen and protected yourself. Thank heavens you're not like Cynthia who fell so madly . . . oh, Marta, you didn't!'

Marta had been unable to stop the tears from coming. She had not cried once over Casmir since coming back to New York and she had prided herself on the strength of her character, but the combination of news from the doctor and Sandra's presence had the effect of undermining her carefully constructed poise. She covered her face to hide her eyes and bent her head towards the table.

'Marta!' Sandra slid next to her and put her arm over Marta's shoulders. 'Not Casmir. You couldn't have.'

'I did,' Marta said, her voice muffled as it came between sobs. 'I didn't mean to.'

'Nobody means to—it just happens. Oh, that lousy, crummy. . . .' and Sandra launched into one of the most creative abuses of the English language that Marta had ever heard. Her curses were so original that Marta could not help smiling despite her tears.

'Where did you learn all that?' she asked, sniffing and lifting her head from her hands.

'I picked it up here and there,' Sandra said, digging a tissue out of her purse. 'Now, blow.'

Marta obediently blew her nose.

'Have you heard from him since he went to San Francisco?'

'No.'

'Well, I haven't heard any gossip that he's picked up someone else, but I don't suppose that's much comfort, is it?'

Marta took another tissue from Sandra and wiped her eyes. 'Tell me your news,' she said. 'Anything has to be better than mine.'

'Mine falls in the jump-in-and-get-your-feet-wet category.'

'Is that good or bad?'

'I don't know.' Sandra gave her a small smile and a shrug. 'I'm leaving the company.'

'Leaving the company!' Marta echoed.

'And moving to Syracuse and. . . .'

'Sandra, you must be joking!'

'I've never been more serious in my life. I called the Director of your old company and got myself a job as a soloist. It's a hell of a lot better than I'll ever do in New York and it will keep me near Steve.'

'I thought you considered your geographic location as an advantage.'

Sandra contemplated her coffee. 'He calls me every night, Marta. I think he misses me.'

Marta sat back and tried to absorb Sandra's words. 'I guess I don't blame you,' she said slowly, 'for going with a regional company. You don't want to be in the corps for the rest of your life.'

'I don't want to be a ballerina for the rest of my life either.'

There was such a tone of bitterness in her voice that Marta gave her a shocked look. 'What does that mean?'

'It means I'm tired of living my life with blinkers on and being brainwashed into thinking that the only thing worth doing is dancing. I want a normal life; a husband and kids and a house. I want to bake cakes and go bicycle riding and be home at night to sit before a fire. I want to *live*,' she finished with vehemence.

Sandra's logic was so heretical that Marta fought back. 'But dancing *is* living. It's wonderful to be up on stage before an audience and bringing to a performance everything that you've trained for. It's. . . .'

'We're the products of the ballet school syndrome,' Sandra said bluntly, 'which means we didn't get much opportunity to think for ourselves. Look at it this way, Marta—from the time we were five or six we've been focused on ballet to the exclusion of everything else. Neither of us really grew up normally; we weren't allowed to act like teenagers—we didn't have boyfriends or go to dances or really learn how to interact with other people. And our ballet teachers nurtured this one-track frame of mind, not giving either of us the chance to learn what other talents we had besides dancing.'

'But I love dancing,' Marta protested.

'So do I,' Sandra said. 'Don't get me wrong, but I know that I can't dance forever—no one can. And I have to be ready to do something else. I have to think about my future and what lies beyond ballet. Steve wants to open a computer store and I plan to take computer courses so I can understand what he's talking about. If the relationship goes the way I'm praying it will, then I want to be prepared for it, not involved in a lifestyle that makes a mockery of marriage.'

'Not a mockery,' Marta objected and cast around for an example. 'Look at Carrie Moore.'

'Carrie has already made choices. She's taken up choreography and started training you to take her place.' Sandra lifted a hand as Marta began to speak. 'Yes, she has. She knows that she can't have babies and maintain her dancing ability. She has a wonderful husband and she isn't about to lose him for a career that's termianl whether she wants it or not. So she's expanded her vision and started to focus on other things. She's lucky that she's creative and can choreograph. I can't so I'm going to have to learn something totally new. It's scary, but I'm excited about it.'

'I can't imagine not dancing,' Marta said in a low voice.

Sandra slapped her hand against the table in frustration. 'Of course, you can't,' she said. 'Did anyone ever encourage you to imagine anything else? No, they cut off every avenue of escape from ballet. The older you got the more hours you trained. If you were like me, you virtually dropped out of high school, right?' At Marta's nod, she continued, 'Don't you see what that training has done to you? You've been taught to believe that there's no other world out there except dancing.'

'But I wanted it that way, too.'

Sandra sighed in acknowledgment. 'I know,' she said. 'It's a mutual arrangement, but think of it this way. It only benefits the company, the critics and the audiences. It doesn't help the dancer because she has nowhere to go when her career comes to an end, and the important point is this: that no one really gives a damn when that happens. There is nothing more useless and discardable to the ballet world than a ballerina who's too old or too injured to dance.'

Later, Marta wished that Sandra's words wouldn't echo and re-echo in her head but they did, over and over again. She had never thought about her training as a dancer in the way Sandra had put it, but she couldn't ignore the other woman's logic. She had thought the years of barre exercise and classes were to teach her body to move to music in a specialised way, never realising that they had also moulded her mind and her thinking. Sandra had called it brainwashing and Marta had to admit to the appropriateness of the term. All her life she had been told that ballet was the only important thing worth doing, and she had swallowed it hook, line and sinker, a willing accomplice in a deception that included her teachers, Madame the Director, Gregory and the other dancers. The ballet school and then the company after it were small, insulated worlds that provided her with a career, friendship, mentors and a goal. She had never needed to look outside; she had found almost everything she wanted in those tight little cliques.

Until now—when she would become what Sandra had described as 'useless' and 'discardable'—the ballerina who could no longer dance. The audiences and critics would forget her, Gregory would replace her with Cynthia and she would be forcibly dropped out of the only society she truly knew. And because she had never prepared herself to be anything else but a dancer, there was no net below Marta to catch her in this precipitous, frightening fall.

For the first time, Marta did not perceive of a future without ballet as a punishment from some angry god. Sandra had compelled her to see it as a wasteland made barren by her own attitude and her own mentality. There were a thousand things she could try her hand at if she had the courage to do so. Money was there if she needed it. She could go to college, open a dance boutique, and marry someone and have children. She could merge with the outside world successfully if she could loosen the hold that dancing had on her. It was an addiction; she recognised that. And, like other addicts, she was going to have to learn how to live without the drug that gave her that dazzling, wonderful high. Marta did not know how she would do it, she only knew that, somehow, she was going to have to find the strength to try.

Support came from a totally unexpected source and in an unexpected way. Simone arrived home from the Caribbean several days before the *Nutcracker* rehearsals were to begin, looking youthful and vigorous with a flattering tan and a new hairstyle.

'Like it?' she asked, revolving before Marta who was seated on the couch in the living room. Simone's luggage was open; her dresses, bathing suits, lounging outfits and gowns draped over every chair and table.

'It's nice.' The hairdresser had cut the pale-red hair shorter than usual and fringed it, giving a soft halo to Simone's face.

'What a lovely trip. I'd promised myself a Caribbean cruise for years.'

'Meet anyone interesting?' The question was phrased casually but it still brought a sharp look from her mother.

'You've never asked me that before.'

'I was just curious.'

Simone paused on her way to the hall, where she had left her suitcases. 'All right—let me put it to you this way. You've never been curious before.'

It hit Marta that her mother was right; she had never been curious about Simone's comings and goings. Oh, she'd enquired if she'd had fun or if a trip had been enjoyable, but she'd never really asked anything personal that went beyond the bounds of polite exchange. But it had just occurred to her as she watched Simone unpack that she had no idea what her mother did for masculine company. She had never dated anyone as far as Marta knew and the idea of her mother bringing a man home was astonishing to her. Yet Simone was young, attractive, vibrant and widowed for thirteen years. No one would condemn her if she had decided to take a lover or remarry again.

'How come you don't date, Mother?'

Simone turned round. 'Is this an inquisition?'

'No.' Marta gave a small shrug. 'It just struck me as odd.'

There was a short silence as Simone sat down in a chair and stared at her hands. She seemed to be coming to some sort of judgment because she took a deep breath, lifted her head and said, 'I have a lover.'

'Really?' Marta was astonished. 'Who?'

'David Graves.'

Of all the men that Marta might have chosen or suspected to be her mother's lover, David Graves came lowest on the list. And it was not because he was not handsome, he was, a tall man who had gone fashionably silver at the temples; or because he was not in her mother's social set; he was a lawyer who was well-connected and well-heeled. It was because David Graves was the husband of her mother's closest and oldest friend in New York, Kay Graves.

'You're kidding,' Marta breathed.

'Ever since your father died. It was one of the reasons I moved to New York when you went to live at the ballet school.'

'But I thought he and Kay were the most attentive couple. They always seemed so close and. . . .'

'It's been a very unhappy marriage, on both sides.'

'Why are they still together?'

Simone shrugged and sighed. 'It's complicated—there's the children and money and family.'

'But if he loves you?'

'Marta, you've never seemed the slightest bit interested in my life or my friends. I really don't understand this sudden and unusual concern.'

But Marta was not to be diverted. 'Do you travel with him? Was he on the cruise?'

'The answer is sometimes and yes.'

Marta thought back over the years her mother had visited one resort and then the next, alighting here and then there in a seemingly indiscriminate fashion. Yet all her travelling had been quite calculated. She must have been meeting David in some of those places when he was free to get away from his wife and his law practice. They could be a couple then, hidden away from public scrutiny, keeping their intimacy discreet and concealed.

'Mother, you're amazing,' Marta said, shaking her head.

'It's not amazing at all—a lot of women do it.'

'Does Kay know?'

'I think Kay suspects, but she has her own life and, for all I know, a lover of her own. We're quite civilised about it.'

Marta shook her head in disbelief. 'It's unbelievable.'

'Just because we're all over fifty doesn't imply that we're not living,' Simone said tartly and then stood up. 'Now, if you're done asking questions, I'll. . . .'

But the moment of intimacy was not to be lost. Marta, who had never before taken the time to understand Simone, was not about to give up this opportunity. 'Were you happy with my father?' she asked.

Simone had turned away from Marta to walk towards the kitchen, but she stopped short and stood perfectly still, her back rigid, her hands clasped together, her face in profile. She was wearing a pale lemon dress and high heels and, for a moment, Marta saw her mother in a totally new perspective. The youthful line of the dress, the softening hair-do and the way the light caught her face seemed to cut the years away, and Marta realised that Simone had been very pretty as a young woman, fine-boned and delicate. Perhaps, even beautiful.

Slowly she turned to face Marta. 'What's behind this?' she asked. 'Why are you asking me all these questions?'

Marta looked down at her bare feet, her toes wiggling in the depth of the plush carpet. 'I've never really understood our family,' she said slowly. 'I never really knew my father at all. That's unusual, isn't it? A daughter not knowing her father?'

'I see,' Simone said slowly.

'And ... I've begun wondering why I became a dancer in the first place.' Simone looked at her so curiously that Marta added, 'I may have to—give it up.'

'Your legs have been bad?'

It was hard to say the words out loud, to hear them spoken in that elegant living room with her mother listening. 'I'll be a cripple if I continue.'

Simone didn't indulge in recriminations or I-told-you-so's. Instead, she walked over to the couch and sat down beside Marta. 'I'm sorry,' she said. 'I know how that must make you feel.'

Marta looked disbelieving; Simone had never been sympathetic about her career. 'Do you?'

'Marta, we've often been at cross-purposes and I make no bones about the fact that I would never have chosen dancing as a career for you. I know that there's glory attached if you make it to the top, but it's a horrible and constricting life. You do nothing but take classes, perform and sleep.'

'I loved it.'

Simone leaned back. 'I know you did. From the

moment you could walk you were dancing around, clapping your hands to music. I thought it was cute then, but I had no idea it would become an obsession. You're so like your father that way. He was such an obsessed person.'

'What do you mean—obsessed?'

'Your father had to be the best in what he did and, if it meant travel, if it meant sacrificing his family to make it to the top, he did that willingly. It's no wonder you didn't know him; he was never home. In the beginning, I chose to stay with you, but when you became so involved with dancing, I was torn in two directions— either to become a ballet mother or try to keep my marriage intact. I chose the marriage instead.'

'I thought you hated what I did.'

'I did hate it. Ballet took you away from me.' Simone mimicked a more youthful Marta. '"Madame says this, Madame says that, Madame says I should take classes ten hours a week, Madame says I'll be a star if I dance more and more and more." You didn't need me, Marta, and you turned away from the sort of things I wanted for you—horseback riding lessons, pretty clothes, boyfriends, college. You devoted yourself to dance.'

Marta had always blamed Simone for their differences; she had always thought her mother was blind to what she had wanted. But her vision of the past had been distorted and coloured by her own perceptions. She had not realised the choices she had forced upon Simone nor had she understood that she might have been difficult and intractable as a child. She had always thought that Simone didn't love her. It had never occurred to her that she might have hurt Simone, turning her childish love in other directions.

In a way, they were both to blame. Another woman with a different personality might have been more sympathetic to a child who was obsessed with dancing. Another woman who was not so interested in the pleasures in life, as Simone admittedly was, might have been willing occasionally to sacrifice those pleasures on the altar of her daughter's ambitions. On the other hand, if Marta had been a different child, she might have given in to Simone more; she might have allowed herself to be dressed up and introduced to her mother's world.

Marta could clearly remember moments when she'd fought Simone right down to the wire, screaming and yelling matches in which she refused to do what her mother wanted her to do; go shopping, visit friends, take an interest in something other than ballet. She'd always had something more important to do—like attend another class or put in extra time at the barre. And, now that Marta thought about it, there was always the shadowy figure of Martin Cole pulling them both in opposite directions. His indifference had helped to fuel her need to dance; she realised now that she had looked for parental praise from her dance instructors, while his obsession with work had forced Simone to a hard decision between spending time with her husband or her daughter. As a family they'd been a dismal failure; broken by differing wants and unable to make compromises. There had been far more to her desire to dance, Marta understood, than merely a love of music and motion.

'I always gave thanks for Peggy and Dave,' Simone was saying, 'although I have to confess to a touch of jealousy. You loved being at their house.'

Marta gave her mother a rueful smile. 'All those toys.'

'And boys.'

'I didn't really want Blaine, you know. I wanted to marry the whole family.'

Simone gave her an understanding look. 'Frankly, I always wondered about that marriage. Blaine was fairly placid, but I wasn't sure he would have put up with your dancing forever.'

'I don't think he would have.'

'Mmm—so what are you going to do now? Have you resigned?'

Marta gazed at her hands which were twisted together in her lap. 'I can't bring myself to do it yet.'

Simone appraised her for a moment and then stood up. 'Well, when you're ready, come to me.' Gently, she placed her hand on Marta's head in a sort of benediction, a blessing that required a few moments of silence, and then she said in a casual tone, 'It strikes me that we have years of catching up to do, don't you think?'

As her mother's hand lifted, Marta raised her head. She was not deceived by the way Simone had spoken these last words—they carried far more import than her tone had warranted. It was a first step in ending the animosity between them, an offer of reconciliation, a statement of her love. 'Yes,' she said slowly. 'I think we do.'

It was surprising to Marta just how important Simone's words came to be to her. As she came closer to making her decision to leave the Manhattan Ballet, the thought of the time she might spend with her mother appeared more desirable and precious. Their relationship was unexplored and untested and yet they had so much in common—a past, memories, certain intimate revelations. Marta was flattered that Simone had confided her affair about David Graves; it was a demonstration of trust that she had not deserved when it was given. For years she had been disinterested in her mother's life and aloof from her cares and concerns. Marta was deeply ashamed of the way she had ignored Simone. She had treated her mother as if she did not exist, as if she did not have feelings, emotions or desires. It struck her as horrendous that she had never once given a thought to her mother's love life assuming, in a totally selfish manner, that Simone had none. Her attitude had helped drive even deeper the wedge that had existed between them.

The pleasure of this new and untried friendship with her mother was the first future happening that Marta could envision without falling into a helpless feeling of depression. Company class had resumed and she attended faithfully, knowing that she would not be coming much longer. With an inertia born of despair and unhappiness, she allowed her name to be put besides Casmir's for the *Nutcracker* even though she knew that her lack of action was irresponsible. She wouldn't be dancing the role of the Sugar Plum Fairy, but she couldn't tell anyone. Sandra was gone, Carrie had taken a winter vacation with Alex and Marta did not have anyone to turn to. It was almost as if she were waiting for a sign, some sort of signal that would indicate to her that her life as a dancer was over.

She learned about Casmir's return to New York one morning from the company bulletin board where the pas de deux rehearsal between the Sugar Plum Fairy and the Nutcracker Prince was listed for that afternoon. Since she had played the part before, Gregory had walked her through it early in rehearsals, remarking that he'd have her practise with Casmir a few times when he came back. She had tried not to think about the moment when she and Casmir would face each other on a dance floor, but she was filled with apprehension. She wondered what he would say to her and how he would act. Perhaps, he'd be merely indifferent, his month's leave having given him time and distance from that evening in the hotel. Perhaps, he would treat her as he treated all the women who had been his lovers—with careless flirtation. Marta didn't think she could stand that, but she knew that she'd have to appear completely impervious, without a flicker of emotion or a hint of vulnerability.

She dressed carefully for the rehearsal, putting on her most tatty leotard, a black one with a ladder on one side seam and shoulder straps that had been patched but still required pins. Her tights were a pale blue colour that had gone greyish from repeated washings; her leg warmers had red and yellow horizontal stripes and were too old to do anything but sink towards her ankles. She wore her most battered point shoes, the ones that had lost most of their satin. When she thought she was appropriate, Marta pulled back her hair in a tight chignon with every hair in place and made up her eyes as if she were going on stage. The woman that stared back at her from the mirror looked the very image of the professional dancer at practice—dramatically made-up and dressed as if she had gone through a rag heap.

Casmir was not in the studio when she arrived. Gregory was pacing the floor, puffing at a cigar, and the pianist was shuffling through her music. Marta put her bag down on the floor and practised a few pliés at the barre before the mirror. Her movements seemed liquid and smooth, but behind the impassivity of her face was the knowledge of pain, not the shooting, stabbing pain that had taken her breath away in *The Sleeping Beauty*, but an ache that originated in her lower back and seemed to seep into her legs. The pain was as steady as Dr Block had predicted it would be when she danced. She was fine when she stood still or walked, but when she turned her hips in the extension that ballet required, her toes pointing outward, it returned in full force. Eventually, he had told her, the pain would be there even when she was not dancing. It would be her constant companion, intensifying and increasing until she would no longer be able to walk or even stand.

She was bending over, her feet in fourth position, her arm gracefully arcing to the floor when she heard Casmir's voice.

'So, Gregory, we do another *Nutcracker*,' he said and Marta slowly, very slowly, pulled herself upright, smoothly extended her arm into second position, a line parallel with her shoulder, and turned her face in his direction.

CHAPTER TEN

MARTA had forgotten how strong the impact of Casmir's masculinity could be. He wore dark practice tights and no shirt, his torso broad and muscular, its lines angling in towards his waist and then flowing into the lean length of his hips and legs. He still had not cut his hair and its blond length was swept back from his temples and ears and waved at his neck. He looked very Russian to her with his wide, high cheekbones and gold-lashed blue eyes. He was smiling but not at her; Gregory was the recipient of that grin, the strong white teeth, carved lips tilted upwards at their ends.

'I can do this one in my sleep,' Casmir said.

Gregory nodded. 'Just a few times with Marta for practice and both of you will have it down perfectly.'

It wasn't until Gregory mentioned her name that Casmir deigned to look at her. His glance took in her very proper ballet stance at the barre, the straight back, regal carriage of head, arm spread wide, her palm up, her fingers slightly curved. She kept her face impassive during this scrutiny, and his gaze seemed to take her in and then discard her as if she were nothing, just another dancer.

Gregory looked from Casmir to Marta in perplexity but then shrugged their problems away. 'Okay,' he said to the pianist, 'start with the opening bars of the pas de deux and take it slowly. We'll speed it up after the first time through.'

Marta was utterly thankful for the years of professional training that enabled her to dance with Casmir, act as light-hearted as the ballet required, smile as if she were enjoying herself thoroughly and not let one flicker of her misery show in her face. She tried to think of Casmir as a partner rather than a lover or the man she had fallen in love with. When his hands spanned her waist or his arm encircled her, she fought against her imagination which conjured up the other times he had touched her. When she felt the deep rise and fall of his chest against hers, she deliberately blacked out the memory of him lying on top of her, the pace of his breathing ragged from passion. She was so successful at this charade that Gregory grunted approval and upped the tempo of the music.

Marta couldn't help seeing that Casmir was equally proficient. He danced brilliantly and with spirit, lifting her and moving her with consummate ease. Marta thought of all the young girls who would fall in love with Casmir as the Nutcracker Prince. He was strong, golden and handsome, and they would feel his magnetism right to the back row of the third balcony. It hurt that none of his warmth and appeal was turned on her, but she hadn't expected anything different. She'd been afraid that he'd be idly flirtatious, but he wasn't. He merely treated her as his partner, smiling at her without a smile in his eyes, his hands gentle and completely indifferent.

This was, Marta came to understand, her last dance. She had received the sign she'd been waiting for, that unknown moment when she would know, beyond the shadow of a doubt, that her career was over. Although she had not planned to actually dance the Sugar Plum Fairy, Marta now realised that underneath she had dreamed that her final curtain call would take place before an audience, their applause acknowledging her skills and her talent, their standing ovation a farewell tribute. Of course, it was the dream of a child or an adolescent—an egocentric fantasy. Reality in the adult world was far different. Marta's last steps were taken in a bare practice room that smelled of sweat with a pianist banging away at a piano that needed tuning, a ballet master who was polluting the air with his cigar and a partner who wouldn't give a damn when she was gone.

The irony of it did not escape her, nor did its pathos. A lifetime of training wiped away in a moment; her dedication no more than a line in a ballet critic's column. In order to save her future, she was sacrificing her past, but few would see it that way. Gregory and Carrie would be sad, but Cynthia would be overjoyed and Casmir clearly would take it in his stride. His genius extended far beyond any particular ballerina; he was a star in his own right. Tears pricked behind Marta's eyes, but she refused to cry in front of anyone. She would save her personal anguish for a private place and time when the enormity of what she had decided hit her.

When the rehearsal ended, everyone left the practice room; the pianist with the music under her arm, Gregory in close conversation with Casmir. Marta was the last to go, and she paused at the threshold of the studio and looked backwards for a long time as if she could absorb the sight of that room with the shaft of light coming in through a high window and the dust motes dancing on its beam. The silence was eerie as if the room waited for that moment when it would be filled with music and the energetic movements of dancers. It seemed just as uncomfortable as Marta felt; awkward and empty and wasted.

She finally turned away and went to her dressing-room where she penned a brief note to Gregory. It was brief and to the point, announcing her resignation for medical reasons, her regret at leaving the company and the hope that her departure would not make scheduling too difficult for him. She wished the company well and hoped that it had years of dancing ahead. She signed her name boldly, blotted it with a tissue and dropped it in the box on Gregory's door. Then she slung her bag over her shoulder, left the building and walked out on to the streets of Manhattan.

Marta walked for hours, the collar of Simone's old fur coat up around her ears to keep her warm and a red beret on her head, her long black hair whipping in the cold breeze. She walked down Fifth Avenue and up

Sixth Avenue. She looked at store windows and theatre marquees; she stared at other pedestrians, and she tried to understand how other people existed, what they did, why they were happy. Only a small proportion of the world were dancers; the rest were storekeepers, housewives, stockbrokers, editors, bankers and chefs. The list of occupations that kept other people busy was endless and Marta, in her wanderings, tried to see herself in these different moulds and wondered if the fit would be tight or easy, pinching or comfortable.

She tried not to think of the world she had left behind, but she wasn't capable of doing so. Little things had a way of reminding her who and what she had been: a poster for a dance company, a type of diet drink that Sandra always drank, a man with broad shoulders and blond hair whose profile took her by surprise until he turned, revealing a narrower and less handsome face than the one she had expected to see.

The thought of Casmir had the ability to deepen Marta's misery to an almost intolerable depth. A man and woman strolling hand-in-hand and a couple kissing by a bus stop were poignant reminders that she was in love with a man who did not want her. She had prepared herself for the worst when she went into rehearsal, but she had got even more than she anticipated. Casual flirtation would have been galling, but at least it would have made her feel as if she existed as a woman. Casmir's aloofness, on the other hand, had given her the feeling that she didn't exist beyond her function as a dancer. His eyes had slid past her; his attentiveness only that demanded of a partner. Beneath her own cool exterior, Marta had prayed that it would be different; that he would enter the studio, his face lighting up when he saw hers, but that was a pipe-dream: another adolescent, romantic fantasy. It had been quite obvious that Casmir would have preferred dancing with someone else and that he intensely disliked the memory of their lovemaking. She had seen that in his eyes and felt it in his hands.

Marta felt as if she'd lost everything; her dancing and the man she loved. Each loss hurt; each made her heart constrict with pain. Ballet had been her life, and Casmir had been her partner. She mourned for both of them with equal intensity, no longer knowing which she grieved for more. She couldn't dance, she couldn't have Casmir. And, even if she could still dance, would she have still wanted to do so without him?

The tears that Marta had tried so hard to hold back overwhelmed her. They ran down her cheeks or were pushed into her temples by the wind. Her eyelashes grew spiky and then icy as dusk approached and the temperature dropped below freezing. She was finally forced to turn towards home; her face growing numb with cold; her legs aching from the walk. Dr Block would have highly approved of the way she had spent the afternoon. 'Walking is the best exercise,' he had said, and Marta thought it ironic that her physical health was at such variance with her mental stability. Her legs felt fine; emotionally, she was drained, exhausted and miserable.

Her nose began running when she entered her apartment building, and she spent the time in the elevator rummaging in her bag for a tissue. She had finally found one when she arrived before the door of the apartment. She was alternately blowing her nose, trying to find her keys and juggling her bag on one hip when the door opened.

'We were wondering where you were,' Simone said. She was made-up for the evening, her hair had been freshly set and she wore a long, blue gown with a diamond choker. Marta remembered that her mother had been invited to dinner and then a show by some friends.

'We?' Marta asked as she entered.

'We have a visitor.'

'Oh.' Marta could not have cared less about company. She put down her bag, finished blowing her nose and then took off her coat.

'Whatever were you up to? You look frozen.'

'I was walking.'

'It's five-thirty.'

'I had a lot to think about. I ... handed in my resignation today.'

'I know, dear.' Simone's voice was gentle. 'He told me.'

Marta looked up and brushed back her hair. 'Who told you?'

Simone gestured towards the living room. 'Casmir. He's been waiting for you.'

He was sitting in Simone's elegant living room on the green velvet chair with its curved legs, a cup of coffee in his hand, its liquid held in the pale bone and rose of her mother's good china. He looked completely out of place in that elegant room with its delicate turn-of-the-century furniture and pale pastel colours. He was wearing a black turtleneck and jeans, and he seemed too large for the chair, his long legs stretched forward, his booted feet crossed at the ankles. Marta didn't think she'd ever seen a man more beautiful. The dark colour set off the sun-gold of his hair and the turquoise of his eyes; the fabric of shirt and jeans clung to his broad muscles.

'Hello,' she said.

Simone was acting the hostess. 'Coffee, darling? I have time to get you a cup before I leave.'

'No, Mother, that's all right.' She sat down opposite him on the couch.

'Casmir? More coffee.'

His voice was deep, almost a rumble. 'No, thank you.'

Simone stood by the couch. 'I wish I could stay longer, but they've scheduled dinner at six and I'm sure you two. . . .' Her voice trailed off as she glanced from Marta to Casmir and then back again. Neither of them was paying her the slightest bit of attention. They were looking at one another, their eyes locked together in silent communication. Simone hesitated and then, giving a helpless and partially amused shrug, walked out of the living room without a word. It wasn't even clear if Casmir and Marta noticed her leaving. They sat in silence until they heard the front door of the apartment shut behind her.

Then Marta spoke. 'Why are you here?'

'Why did you resign?' Casmir countered.

'Because I couldn't dance anymore.'

'That injury?'

'It isn't an injury,' Marta said. 'It's a condition. I've had it since the accident and the doctor says it will get worse if I continue dancing.'

A look of understanding passed over his face. 'That was why you were so angry in Syracuse after the *The Sleeping Beauty*. You were afraid I would find out and stop you from dancing.'

'It was my decision to make.'

'So,' he mused, 'I was right then.'

She lifted her chin. 'You were right.'

The news that his opinion had been confirmed didn't seem to make Casmir happy. He glowered at her, the dark-gold of his eyebrows forming a straight line across his brow. 'Why do you not say this in rehearsal today?'

Marta could hardly tell Casmir the truth. She couldn't say what she had learned in rehearsal—that dancing in pain was nothing to dancing without love, but she could not bear the thought of being in Casmir's arms when he didn't want her, and that she could no longer imitate the gestures of love as she danced, knowing how loveless their partnering was. So she gave him an evasive answer. 'I didn't want to make a scene,' she said. 'I preferred to resign by letter.'

Casmir put down his cup. 'So you never dance again,' he said slowly. 'I am sure this is upsetting to you.'

Did he have to rub her nose in the fact? Did he have to flaunt his health before her? Marta sprang up, her face flushed with anger, her hands clenched at her sides. 'I don't see that it matters to you,' she said through gritted teeth.

Casmir also stood up, his lean height suddenly menacing. 'You don't think I care when I lose a partner?'

'There's a thousand ballerinas who are just dying to dance with you.'

'Perhaps I don't want them.'

'You'll find someone,' she said.

They glared at one another; fury making Marta feel as if she were on fire while Casmir merely grew more still, his eyes narrowing. 'So you end it, just like that,' he said, snapping his fingers in demonstration.

'Just like that,' she agreed.

'You walk away and do not look back.'

How dare he imply that she had no regrets and no feelings about the end of her dancing career? She was crying inside; she felt as if she were being torn apart, and he was suggesting that her decision was careless and unemotional. So great was her rage that, if Marta had been able to fight at that moment, she would have strangled him with her bare hands. *He* was the one who could walk away, leave her naked and trembling on a bed and act as if nothing had occurred between them.

'Yes,' she said, flinging the word at him. 'Just like you.'

'Like me?' He watched her suspiciously. 'What does that mean?'

'Any man who can walk out on a woman after ... after. ...'

'After she cries because he makes love to her? Because he is not her husband?' Suddenly Casmir was standing in front of her, looking down at her, the turquoise eyes blazing. 'Because he reminds her of a bad one-night stand?'

'If you had stayed. ...' she began.

He grabbed her by the shoulders and shook her. 'You know how it feels to make love to you knowing that your mind is with another man?'

'It wasn't,' she protested.

'No?'

'No, I never even thought of Blaine or that other man.'

'Then why do you cry as if your heart is breaking?'

Marta couldn't answer. She simply looked up at him.

'Why?' he said harshly, his hands tightening on her shoulders into a painful grip. 'I think about this all the time I am in San Francisco.' She could see the muscle clenching and unclenching in his jaw; she could feel the powerful anger in his hands. The tension between them was so strong that Marta could feel the heavy thudding of her heart, the racing of her blood to her pulse. 'I think that this love we make together is so perfect and so honest but when we are done, you cry.'

A sudden happiness gripped Marta so hard that her breath was taken away. She could hear the anguish in Casmir's voice, feel it in his hands, see it in his eyes. She had believed that he had walked away and gone to San Francisco without a thought about her; she had been convinced that he cared no more about her than he had cared for Cynthia or the endless procession of ballerinas who had danced their way through his life and his bed. But he hadn't been indifferent at all. He had suffered at her hands the way she had suffered at his. She could feel his pain—feel it in the way he was convulsively gripping her shoulders, his fingers digging into her arms.

'I want you to tell me,' he grated. 'I want to know why.'

Marta took a deep, shaky breath and plunged in. 'Because ... it was so wonderful and I'd never felt anything like that before.' She stopped but he remained silent; his glittering blue gaze locked into hers. Marta swallowed and went on, 'Because I realised that I didn't know what lovemaking really meant and I'd no idea that anyone ... that a man ... that you could. ...' She could no longer speak, not because she had lost any facility with words, but because Casmir had pulled her up to him and buried his face in her hair.

'Marta, Marta,' he crooned, wrapping his arms

around her, rocking slightly from one side to the other and repeating her name over and over again as if it were a mantra. 'Marta.'

She didn't think she'd ever felt anything so glorious in her life as Casmir's bear hug. He was holding her so tightly that her breath came short and her bones felt like they might crack, but she loved every sensation; his mouth against her ear, his chest crushed to hers, his hand caressing her back in long sweeps. 'Casmir?' she whispered and touched her hand to his hair in a gesture of wonderment.

He lifted his head and looked down at her. 'Marta, why didn't you say this? Why did you let me think that you regretted sleeping with me?'

'You didn't give me a chance. You left too quickly.'

He groaned. 'I do not sleep for a whole month, *milaya*, I do not eat, I walk up and down the streets of San Francisco. I wonder what has happened between us; I try to think what it is I have done so that you should cry. . . . Damn, you are crying again!'

Marta couldn't help it, the tears were flowing out of her, but they were a product of happiness and they felt cleansing. 'I've been crying for a whole month,' she admitted. 'Soon I won't have any tears left.'

Gently he wiped her cheek with his thumb. 'I promise, you will not have to cry anymore. I will spend hours in bed with you, I will make more love to you. You will smile, *lapushka*, not cry.'

She wrapped her arms around his neck. 'Oh, Casmir,' she said. 'It sounds wonderful.'

They kissed then, a long, sweet entanglement of mouths, lips and tongues, a kiss that held the glory of the moment and the promise of the future. They drank from one another's mouths as if they were dying of thirst, and when they parted, both Casmir and Marta smiled at one another.

'I think I tie you to a bed,' Casmir said in mock-warning.

'And I wondered what I'd be doing when I stopped

dancing.' Marta spoke in a light and teasing tone, and then realised with surprise that the words had, for the moment, lost their sting.

But Casmir took her words seriously. 'Ah, *lyubimaya*, I am broken-hearted. I don't want to dance with anyone else.'

She couldn't resist teasing him. 'Not even Cynthia?'

'Cynthia,' he said with disgust. 'She is dancer, but she is not you.'

'Carrie will be back.'

He sighed gloomily. 'Carrie is marvellous, but she is no longer so interested in dancing.'

'There will be others,' Marta said gently.

'But I do not love these others.' Casmir pulled her up to him and touched his mouth softly on hers. 'I find this out in San Francisco—that I have loved you for a long time, Marta. And when I come back and see you in rehearsal and you are so cold and distant, I think that part of my heart dies.'

'But you were cold to me,' she protested. 'You were terrible.'

'I was afraid,' he confessed. 'Afraid that you hate me for what I had done to you.'

'I love you,' she said. 'I could never hate you.'

He gazed deeply into her eyes. 'And you will marry me?' he asked.

Marta blinked in bewilderment. Their mutual declaration of love had been so wonderful that the thought of marriage had not even entered her head. 'Marry you?'

He stepped back and let go of her. 'You do not want this?'

'Well I hadn't given it much. . . .'

'I do not want a lover, I want a wife.' She stared at him, surprised by his vehemence. 'Marta, I have more lovers than I care to mention. They are easy to find and easy to discard. But this does not make me happy anymore. I need a woman who is mine and children to make my house a home. Bonnie did not want to give me sons and daughters, but I think you are different. I pray for this: that you will marry me and bring me children.'

The image of the babies that she and Casmir would create together made a lump come into Marta's throat. 'Yes,' she whispered. 'Oh, yes.' The next minute, she was being lifted with a bewildering speed, one of Casmir's arms around her back, the other under her knees as he swung her upwards against his chest. 'Casmir, what are you doing?' she asked in alarm, throwing her arms around his neck to keep her balance, her dark hair tumbling against his shoulder.

'We start immediately, *lapushka*.'

'Start what?'

'Making babies. It is not such an easy job, it requires practice.' He strode out of the living room and into the hallway. 'Which way is your bedroom?'

'Not now!' she protested.

Casmir stopped and looked down at her. 'Why not? You have a previous engagement?' She shook her head. 'Another lover? No? You are hungry for dinner? You have religious objections?'

Marta was laughing and could hardly speak. 'Religious objections?'

Casmir shrugged. 'Perhaps you do not make love on Tuesdays—only Mondays, Thursdays and Sundays.'

'God, I missed you,' she said, loving the look he was giving her, the smile in his blue eyes, the laughter that curved his lips upward, the dimple in one cheek.

'We correct that condition,' he promised and kissed her on the tip of her nose.

When he brought her into the bedroom, the afternoon light had almost completely disappeared, leaving the corners of the room in shadow and turning the dark green quilt almost black. One small lamp was lit on a table and it threw a fan of illumination that picked up the brass gleam of the headboard and deepened the glowing red and gold of several throw pillows. It was into this pool of light that Casmir gently laid Marta on the bed. He pulled off her shoes and, sitting down next to her, spread her hair out on the pillow so her face seemed a small white oval set off in a black halo. 'For a whole month, I dream of taking you to bed,' he said, his tone almost reverent, 'but I do not have any hope that you will ever let me touch you again. I truly believe this is a miracle, Marta, that I am here with you.' And solemnly, he lifted her hand to his mouth and placed his lips on her palm.

Marta felt the brand of his kiss burning her skin, and the blood beneath it carried the message of his passion through her veins and to her heart, which began to beat in a slow and heavy rhythm. Her breath seemed to come short as desire moved within her, curling and uncurling, spreading a sensual warmth into her legs, her arms and the delicate skin of her face. Her cheeks glowed as she looked up at him, her eyes dark-blue and shining.

'Is it true that you do not think of your husband when I am with you?' he asked.

Marta shook her head. 'Blaine was like a brother to me. I married him for his family and called it love.'

'And this is why you don't have any children with him?'

'I. . . .' Marta paused as she considered Casmir's words. 'I didn't want to have children, but I thought the fault was mine—that I was too selfish and too obsessed with my own career to take time out for a family. Perhaps it wasn't that, perhaps I didn't want to have children with him because I really didn't love him or because underneath I knew that we were really children ourselves playing house. We fought about it a lot and . . . and, on the night he died, we argued about having children again. That's why we had the accident . . . because he didn't see a truck, and the car swerved on the ice and. . . .'

Her voice had risen to a tense and shrill level, her body gone rigid with the memory, and Casmir stretched out beside her and pulled her into his arms. 'Hush,' he said, 'you must not blame yourself.'

'But if I hadn't been arguing with him, it wouldn't have happened!'

'Marta, he argued with you, too.'

'But it's my fault, don't you see? If I'd agreed with him, then. . . .'

'But you couldn't.'

'No, but if only . . .' Marta took a deep, shuddering sigh. 'There's so many "if onlys".'

'You have been punished enough, *milaya*. You have lost your dancing.'

Marta looked up at him and saw understanding in his eyes. A weight seemed to lift off her, the burden of guilt and of shame. Blaine had accused her of being selfish and she had believed him, not realising then that part of her reluctance to have children arose from the lack of real love that she bore him. Marta was not the type to believe in divine retaliation, and Casmir was right—she surely had suffered enough. A wonderful sense of absolution came to her, a cleansing and purifying release from guilt.

'Thank you,' she whispered.

'For what?'

'For telling me that.'

Casmir rolled on to his back, kicked off his boots so that they hit the carpeted floor with a dull thud, and pulled Marta around until her head rested on the soft indentation of his shoulder. She could hear the faint drumming of his heart beneath her ear and feel the steady rise and fall of his chest. 'I know about these things,' he said slowly. 'I have lived with Bonnie's death in my heart and head for years. She was killed going to a store for some spices I needed.'

'Carrie told me about it,' she said softly.

Casmir stared up at the ceiling. 'I say to myself, over and over again, that I should have gone instead, that no mugger would have attacked me. I start to drink from thinking like this, and I almost lose my dancing. Then it comes to me that this event cannot be foreseen, that no one can understand why it happens, and I must not punish myself for it. Which is not to say that my heart eases forever. There is always somewhere inside of me a feeling of blame. I think I will die with it.'

'You loved her,' Marta said.

'This makes you jealous, *lapushka*?'

'A bit.'

Casmir ran a caressing hand over her hair. 'You are so different than Bonnie. She was hard and glittery and tough. You are softer and there is a sweetness in you that she did not have. And Bonnie and I fought so much that she took my energy away; sometimes I wonder if we were meant to be lovers rather than husband and wife. But I don't think this about you; I believe that we will have a better marriage. And you must never doubt how I feel about you. I love you deeply.'

Marta wrapped her arms around Casmir's waist and hugged him tight. 'Can I make a confession?'

'Anything.'

'I'll hate every woman you dance with,' she confessed.

'I will not care about them.'

'But they'll be sharing a part of your life that I can't have.'

'And you will have a part they will never see. I know you will miss ballet; I understand this, but I want you to fill up your life with other things.'

She couldn't resist teasing him. 'Like you, for instance?'

Casmir kissed the top of her head. 'Of course,' he said in the same light-hearted vein and then added more seriously, 'and children. I meant what I said, Marta, I would like some soon.'

'I want children, too,' she said, 'but I'd like to do something else as well. I've watched Carrie, and I know that full-time motherhood would get me down.'

'Marta, life is waiting for you with open arms.'

Casmir was right, of course. Now that she had finally turned her mind away from dancing, Marta could see that the future held possibilities that she'd never envisioned before. She hadn't quite believed Sandra's theory about the way the ballet world suffocated its dancers, but she was beginning to realise that her vision had been so focused and so intent on dancing that she had been, in a metaphorical sense, wearing blinkers so that she wouldn't be distracted by the enticements and attractions of the outside world.

It beckoned to her now as a glittering vista, and Marta was aware that Casmir had changed her perspective. She knew that she had looked for affection from her dance teachers because it was an emotion lacking in her family, but she had never realised that ballet had acquired for her a much stronger and more symbolic meaning. Dance had served as a surrogate parent for her; the audiences had acted as replacements for the parents she had never known. It was no wonder that she'd grown so addicted to performing; she had felt the applause and ovations as vast outpourings of love. Nothing had ever seemed so wonderful and exciting as those moments when she was bent in a deep curtsey, the sounds of thousands of clapping hands directed only at her.

But being loved by Casmir took away that driving need, that frantic urgency she'd had to dance. She no longer needed the praise of a ballet master or a mention by a dance critic or a theatre filled with strange faces to feel good inside. Just the thought of marriage to Casmir made her feel happy. There would be the wedding, the honeymoon, an apartment to furnish, a new life to adjust to and, perhaps, an early pregnancy. She'd have time to do things she'd never had the leisure to do before; read, go to shows, see museums, explore the city, spend time with Simone. She could discover the terrain that existed beyond ballet; the studio and the stage, the constant training and rehearsals. Marta knew that a part of her would always deeply regret the end of her dancing, but another part of her was waking up, like an animal that had been long in hibernation, and it was as curious and eager and as wide-eyed as a young child.

'Perhaps I'll write a novel about ballet,' she said in idle speculation. 'About what it's like to be a dancer.'

'That sounds good.'

She smiled into his shoulder. 'And maybe I'll add a sexy partner for fun.'

'Oh?' Casmir said with a growl.

'He's handsome and impetuous.'

'Yes?'

'And he sweeps the ballerina off her feet.'

'And right into her bed?'

'Casmir,' Marta said scoldingly. 'you have a one-track mind.'

'When you are with me, I can think of nothing else. *Nothing.*' He wrapped one hand gently around her throat and lifted her chin with his thumb so that she could neither move her head nor turn away from his gaze. The light burnished his hair a molten gold, and was reflected in the blue of his eyes as dancing flames. 'I want you,' he said huskily, 'more than anything I have ever wanted in my life. Do you understand this?'

'Yes,' she whispered.

'And I take you now and with love?'

'Yes.'

'And you will not cry?'

Marta smiled slightly. 'I can't promise that.'

'Then my tears will mix with yours, *milaya*, and we cry together. Always together.' He reached beyond her and flicked off the lamp, throwing them into the shadows of dusk. His lips touched hers then; at first lightly as if in reverence, and then more passionately as if in promise of what was to come. And Marta discovered that, beyond ballet, there existed a dance of love and it was far more exquisite and far more meaningful than anything she had ever danced before.

Just what the woman on the go needs!

BOOKMATE

The perfect "mate" for all Harlequin paperbacks!

Holds paperbacks open for hands-free reading!

- TRAVELING
- VACATIONING
- AT WORK • IN BED
- COOKING • EATING
- STUDYING

Perfect size for all standard paperbacks, this wonderful invention makes reading a pure pleasure! Ingenious design holds paperback books OPEN and FLAT so even wind can't ruffle pages—leaves your hands free to do other things. Reinforced, wipe-clean vinyl-covered holder flexes to let you turn pages without undoing the strap...supports paperbacks so well, they have the strength of hardcovers!

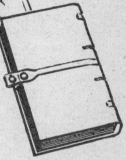

Snaps closed for easy carrying.

Available now. Send your name, address, and zip or postal code, along with a check or money order for just $4.99 + .75¢ for postage & handling (for a total of $5.74) payable to Harlequin Reader Service to:

Harlequin Reader Service

In the U.S.A.
2504 West Southern Ave.
Tempe, AZ 85282

In Canada
P.O. Box 2800, Postal Station A
5170 Yonge Street,
Willowdale, Ont. M2N 5T5

MATE-1R

Take these 4 best-selling novels FREE

ANNE MATHER
born out of love

VIOLET WINSPEAR
time of the temptress

CHARLOTTE LAMB
man's world

SALLY WENTWORTH
say hello to yesterday

Take these
4 best-selling novels
FREE

Yes! Four sophisticated,
contemporary love stories
by four world-famous
authors of romance
FREE, as your
introduction to the Harlequin Presents
subscription plan. Thrill to **Anne Mather**'s
passionate story BORN OUT OF LOVE, set
in the Caribbean.... Travel to darkest Africa
in **Violet Winspear**'s TIME OF THE TEMPTRESS....Let
Charlotte Lamb take you to the fascinating world of London's
Fleet Street in MAN'S WORLD .... Discover beautiful Greece in
Sally Wentworth's moving romance SAY HELLO TO YESTERDAY.

*The very finest
in romance fiction*

Join the millions of avid Harlequin readers all over the
world who delight in the magic of a really exciting novel.
EIGHT great NEW titles published EACH MONTH!
Each month you will get to know exciting, interesting,
true-to-life people . . . . You'll be swept to distant lands you've
dreamed of visiting . . . . Intrigue, adventure, romance, and
the destiny of many lives will thrill you through each
Harlequin Presents novel.

Get all the latest books before they're sold out!
As a Harlequin subscriber you actually receive your
personal copies of the latest Presents novels immediately
after they come off the press, so you're sure of getting all
8 each month.

Cancel your subscription whenever you wish!
You don't have to buy any minimum number of books.
Whenever you decide to stop your subscription just let us
know and we'll cancel all further shipments.

Your **FREE** gift includes

Anne Mather—Born out of Love
Violet Winspear—Time of the Temptress
Charlotte Lamb—Man's World
Sally Wentworth—Say Hello to Yesterday

Mail this coupon today!

FREE Gift Certificate
and subscription reservation

Harlequin Reader Service

In the U.S.A.
2504 West Southern Ave.
Tempe, AZ 85282

In Canada
P.O. Box 2800, Postal Station A
5170 Yonge Street,
Willowdale, Ont. M2N 6J3

Please send me my 4 Harlequin Presents books free. Also, reserve a subscription to the 8 new Harlequin Presents novels published each month. Each month I will receive 8 new Presents novels at the low price of $1.75 each [*Total—$14.00 a month*]. There are no shipping and handling or any other hidden charges. I am free to cancel at any time, but even if I do, these first 4 books are still mine to keep absolutely FREE without any obligation. 108 BPP CAGC

NAME   (PLEASE PRINT)

ADDRESS   APT. NO.

CITY

STATE/PROV.   ZIP/POSTAL CODE

This offer is limited to one order per household and not valid to current *Harlequin Presents* subscribers. We reserve the right to exercise discretion in granting membership.
Offer expires September 30, 1985
® ™ Trademarks of Harlequin Enterprises Ltd.   P-SUB-3US

If price changes are necessary you will be notified.